"I received a letter."

"Yes, go on. Speak plainly."

"It was from Edward Teache. He asked for my hand in marriage."

Lucian stood so quickly it knocked her off balance. She was taken aback as he paced to and fro across the school room floor, muttering. "This will not do. No this will not do at all."

"Lucian—"

"How long have you known this?" His eyes went wild and pupils became a pinprick. His dark hair fell across his forehead and he swiped it out of his face in irritation.

"A-about two weeks...I was going to tell you, but I did not want to intrude on our happiness."

"Stanzy, obviously you do not realize the gravity of this situation. Teache is very dangerous; I did not want you to know *how* dangerous as I did not want to alarm you—"

"Alarm *me*? Someone who has been caring for herself and two siblings—one a mere baby—since she was sixteen years old? Who traveled across the Atlantic without male escort? I do not need your protection, I need your honesty!"

"And I yours!" He stormed out of the school, throwing the door open so hard it hit the wooden frame with an earsplitting clatter.

The Bride

of

Blackbeard

Brynn Chapman

Highland Press Publishing
Florida

The Bride of Blackbeard

For information, please contact
Highland Press Publishing,
PO Box 2292, High Springs, FL 32655.
www.highlandpress.org

ISBN: 978-0-9800356-3-6

HIGHLAND PRESS PUBLISHING

Americana

Dedication

To Ron, Sandy and Ryan Chapman, for all you have done.

And in loving memory of Delvin Ellwood and Dorothy Chapman, your struggles and triumphs will never be forgotten.

Acknowledgement

Sincere thanks to my agent, Lois Bennett,
for supporting my work, and to the
excellent literary judgment of my editor,
Patty Howell, for always helping turn words
to polished fiction.

~ *Chapter One* ~

July 1718

> *I cannot let him strike me again. I am going mad from it.*

Her father's massive fist darted out and connected with her cheek. Pain exploded in her face and her knees buckled. She landed on the floor in a heap. Stunned, she lifted her hand, staring in horror at her father, and felt a welt rising on her cheek.

His fingers were round as sausages—the hands of a butcher, not a surgeon.

"I hate you and your cursed sister, and yes, even the boy," he growled. "I regret the day I ever lay with your mother. She has gone and left me with what? A heart that will not mend, and three mouths to feed; I ask you—how can that be fair?"

Constanza slowly raised her head, hoping she wouldn't have the vertigo. She didn't. Not this time. She gazed out at the rising sun. *If I tell him what I really think, this will escalate into an all out brawl. Soon, Kitty and William will rise, and then they will see it. Stay down, do not speak. Hold your tongue...but I so want to tell him what a miserable drunken lark of a father he is...No, do not rise.*

With much effort, she forced a look of calm on her face. "You have patients in less than two hours and you have just returned home. I suggest you go have a lie, or we will be turning away our day's wages."

Constanza woke from the dream and looked around. *I have traded one nightmare for another.*

She regarded the bowels of the ship, which contained the chattel. As the ship cut through the swells, every board creaked in protest. A small girl of six lay curled up against her mother for warmth—the child's father had passed on yesterday. Constanza watched as the little girl's hand covered her mouth, desperately trying not to wretch at the fetid stench that filled the air.

The sound of gunfire exploded nearby; close enough to render Constanza deaf for a moment. She bolted upright and purposely began to open and close her mouth, all the while sticking her fingers in her ears in some stupid, sleep-filled attempt to restore her hearing.

She looked to her left, searching for her sister, and saw Katrina moving behind her, as she had since the day she was born.

"Where is William?" Constanza shouted.

"I do not know," Katrina replied.

Constanza stood and fought the ever-present light-headedness that always occurred the morning after a full night to and fro on the Brigantine ship.

Once the dizziness subsided, her nostrils were assailed with the next onslaught. The stench—an over-whelming miasma of human misery. The future colonists were wedged in between crates of unknown contents. The smell from the combination of their inability to cleanse themselves properly, and vomit from those who were still unable to get their sea legs, presented a cauldron of pestilence.

She wound her way through the sea of bodies, trying not to stare at the half dead, newly dead, or pitifully sick.

What was I thinking? America, humph. We would have been better off on the streets of Bristol than to die on this floating cesspool before even stepping foot on North Carolina soil.

"William!" she bellowed. "Where are you?"

She began to climb the ladder to the deck, where seamen only permitted 'the cargo' out from the hold two times a day, but she didn't care.

If they shoot me now, at least the suffering will be over. A quick death would be preferable to enduring the rest of this voyage.

Careful to mind the rigging, she walked around the deck. Her eyes darted so frantically she feared she'd vomit on the spot and draw attention to herself. The few crew members who'd spied her leered almost uncontrollably. After ninety days at sea, it amazed her only two rapes had occurred. Purposefully, she cast her eyes downward, so as not to encourage them. She didn't plan on becoming another victim of morally destitute men.

Then she saw him. William stood at the bow of the ship with the captain. As she approached, she could see many rope knots lying about the deck. A figure eight knot laid at Will's feet and a partially constructed slip knot in his hand.

"No offense, Captain. But I am of the mind William would be better off learning how to use a spade and a plow as we are destined for North Carolina."

The man looked up from William. Even in the dawn's light, the captain was a menacing creature. His full head of black hair and shaggy mane of a beard made him appear more animal than man. However, he had looked after her family since they'd boarded his vessel. Captain Teache took a particular interest in Will. But she wasn't a fool. This was merely a ruse for his real interest—herself or her sister.

And let us be realistic; between me and Katrina, there is no contest. Katrina has always been the fairest.

Arranged by her ailing uncle for a much decreased fare, the captain had agreed to take the three of them to the *New World*. After a lifetime toiling at sea, the captain was to become a gentleman of leisure. On more than one occasion, Teache had expressed that this was his first and *last* voyage with passengers. An agreement had been reached through Charles Eden, Governor of North Carolina. All misfits had been allowed passage to the outer banks—the barrier islands that protected a major portion of the coastline of the North Carolinian colony.

"Come, Will. You have troubled the captain long enough."

As she slipped her arm around her eleven-year-old brother's shoulders, she felt the eyes of every crew member on her, making the hairs on the back of her neck stand on end.

"It will be a miracle if we make it to North Carolina," she whispered into William's ear.

In the ship's hold, Constanza's foot jerked in response to her dream, connecting with William's backside. She slept as much as possible since she could never escape the seasickness. He pushed her leg out of his back and rolled away.

Constanza! Get in here right now!" her father bellowed.

She sat on the side of her bed and trembled.

"Stanzy!" It came again through the floorboards.

Her door cracked open and her mother poked her head in, squinting through the gloom.

"Constanza, honey? Are you awake?"

"Yes, Mama. I don't want to go down. He has been drinking again, hasn't he?"

Her mother bit her lip, her dark-circled, hollow eyes staring at Constanza. She moved to the end of the bed, picked up Constanza's chemise and folded it. "Yes, dear, he has, but he is trying to overcome it. Three months have passed since he has been this way."

Stanzy sat for a moment trembling, from rage instead of fear.

"For mercy's sake, Mother, he is a surgeon and a drunk! A worse combination than any I can think of. Yet you expect me to go down and assist him again?"

"Constanza, you know you are his favorite."

"I am a substitute for the son he so desperately wants. And the only reason he has taught me everything he knows is for occasions like this, not out of concern for how I will make my way in this world."

A woman's screams wafted up through the floorboards, echoing in the huge old manor.

The door opened again and tiny Katrina entered

rubbing her eyes, *"Momma, I'm scared."* Her petite arms encircled her mother's legs.

Her mother turned and looked at her eldest daughter, desperation on her face, and whispered, *"Please..."*

Constanza hung her head and squeezed her eyes tightly shut...*"For you, Mama. Only for you."*

She made her way down the back steps—the servants' stairwell, if they had still possessed any— opening the door to her father's operating room. The stale smell of old spirits smacked her in the face and she wondered how the woman on the table hadn't already been anesthetized.

"What is it, Father?"

"What took you so long, child? She is ten centimeters dilated and the baby is not progressing down the birth canal. What will be your course of action?"

Constanza moved to the foot of the bed and peered between the pair of open legs. She could see the crown of the baby's head. The mother was lying still, however, as Stanzy watched a huge contraction hit her belly. The woman made no sound or movement.

"Father, did you give her laudanum? How will she be any use to us now to extract this child? And each time you have done it in the past, the babies are groggy and never feed well the first few days."

"She was screaming and I could not concentrate," he slurred.

"I am sure the Scotch had absolutely nothing to do with it," she hissed under her breath.

"Pigeon, let us not squabble, there is work to be done."

Constanza walked to the side of the bed and held up the woman's legs to attempt to widen the birth canal. Dr. Smythe stumbled to the foot of the bed and blinked, attempting to focus on the baby's head. He rubbed his eyes and ran a hand down his whiskered chin.

Gently setting down the woman's legs, Constanza reached behind her, snatched up a glass of water and threw the cold liquid straight into her father's bleary *face.*

He shook his head back and forth, lucidity returning to his features.

Another contraction hit and hardened the belly, but the woman didn't stir.

"How much did you give her? What if her labor stops? The baby will die."

"No, they are coming hard and steady every minute. Look, here is another one!"

The rounded belly rose with another rippling contraction. Grabbing the other leg, Stanzy angled her arm, applying downward pressure to assist the child's descent along the birth canal.

"That is it, my darling. It is coming now." As if on cue, the sound of Dr. Smythe collapsing to the floor echoed through the now quiet house.

Constanza raced to the end of the bed, and in concert with the next contraction placed her fingers in beside the head. The child slid into her arms in a rush of fluid. Swaddling the child with the birthing blanket, she gently rocked him. A soft, cat-like mewling issued from the child.

Her eyes fell to the new mother, lying on the table, sleeping the blissful dreams of laudanum, then to her drunken father at her feet. She watched as if outside herself as tears dropped from the end of her nose, dotting the baby's blanket.

Finally opening her eyes, she felt displaced in time. She blinked and rubbed them in an attempt to get her bearings. She dug inside the pocket of her shift. *Where is it?* Relief flooded her body when her hand grasped the cold steel of the knife she'd hidden.

William, Katrina?

With both hands she searched in the dark for her siblings, sighing when she felt their warm, soft skin. Both snored softly despite the despicable surroundings. They had started the voyage with fifty men, women and children and now thirty remained. By her calculations, they'd been tossed to and fro at sea for one hundred days, with approximately twenty more to go.

Will's Sheep dog snuggled peacefully at his side. She thought it highly unusual that they'd been permitted passage for the dog. More than likely, she reasoned, it was because the seamen would probably kill and devour him if grave circumstances arose.

I do not want to dream again. I am not sure which is worse, being home in the past or here on this rubbish vessel.

Quietly standing, she stole away from the sleeping trio, and headed again for fresh air. During the day, she was able to make peace with her woeful upbringing, but at night the wars battled on inside her damaged mind.

As she made her way up the ladder, a pair of legs dangled into the hole—pretty, shapely legs—which was most likely the reason why this person was being permitted to take this perch by the most dishonorable seamen—so that they might enjoy the view.

Of course, she knew the girl—like she knew everyone below deck now. Her name was Amelia and she was traveling to the Carolinas with her parents in hope of making a new start.

"Allo, Amelia. Couldn't sleep either?"

"No. I come up here most every night to get a bit of the breeze, and the boys, they never tell me to go..."

"No, I do not expect they do." Constanza leaned over and whispered, "A young lady as beautiful as you ought to be careful around sailors starved of female attention."

Amelia blushed, tossing a long curl over her shoulder. "You really think I am beautiful?"

Clearly, the meaning of the entire conversation, what Constanza was trying to convey, was lost to this girl. Amelia was about Katrina's age and they'd become fast friends. Both were fifteen, beautiful and obsessed with men and finding husbands.

Due to an unusual upbringing, Constanza had very little use for men. Since the age of twelve, her father had trained her to become a surgeon's assistant. As such, she'd witnessed more births, deaths, illnesses and plague than any female she'd ever known. Her mother had been interested in herbology—what some folks referred to as a natural healer. When Constanza's father found standard medicinal therapies ineffective, he would often consult with his wife as to what herbs had what properties to assist his problem patients.

Their entire small yard in Bristol had housed a tremendous herb garden, which Stanzy had been expected to learn, and had. She'd shouldered the burdens of the family instead of her mother, who'd spent her entire life trying to keep her family together despite her husband's drinking. Although her mother was decidedly weak, Stanzy had once asked her, near the end of her life, why she'd stayed. Her mother's chilling answer was one that rang in her ears to this very day.

"Where would we have gone, child?"

Constanza's only meaningful relationship with a man of substance had been her mother's brother, Delvin Ellwood Channing. Uncle Delvin had given her advice since the time she was old enough to walk.

He'd arranged this journey for all of them. She could still see her dear uncle's hands shake as he perused the list of debts her father had hidden from her. He'd presided over the sale of their manor to keep her from debtor's prison, and her siblings from the workhouse.

Another flip of Amelia's blonde curls brought Constanza out of her reverie. The girl was peering around at the few seamen who were awake and smiling fetchingly at them.

Constanza shivered at the sexual tension on the deck. "Amelia, do you remember the women who were taken up on deck, and did not return?"

"Yes, my parents' said they fell ill and died." Her full lips pouted.

"No, dear, the crewmen forced themselves on them, in the husbandly way. Then I believe they were killed. They had no family to speak for them."

"No!" Her doe eyes grew huge and clearly afraid now.

"Yes, so let us not sit here and draw attention to

16

ourselves more than necessary."

"Yes, yes. All right."

Constanza snickered despite herself as Amelia slumped her shoulders in a feeble attempt to hide her plump breasts.

"So, what is tempting a woman of your age to the colonies, Miss Constanza Smythe?"

"A woman of my age, which is twenty and eight, by the by, is taking the post of governess to two children on a plantation in North Carolina. My uncle arranged it for us, allowing Will and Kitty to come along with me, which is certainly not the custom. My uncle was able to find a family who would take us; I guess they'd had some difficulties with past governesses."

"Oh, you will make a fine governess. My father always says spinsters make the best..." She stopped, evidently realizing in her self-centered adolescent way perhaps spinster wasn't the most favorable or courteous term.

Constanza smiled. "Have you heard any tales about Currituck County?"

"No, ma'am. I do not read the written word. My father says it is indecent for young women. What have you heard?" She leaned close, hopeful that the gossip from Currituck was as juicy as that of Bristol.

"The word Currituck comes from the native word for Wild Goose. And of course Dare County is named after Virginia Dare, the first child born in the New World."

She watched Amelia's eyes glaze over much like Katrina's would when given a history lesson. Amelia was much more interested in vivid detailed descriptions of the latest frocks from France, or who had married whom last Sunday.

"Have you ever heard of Nags Head?"

Amelia nodded.

"My uncle is a retired merchant sailor. He recently told me the people of Nags Head are tiring of all of the rumrunning through their ports, so they have devised a scheme to acquire some of the profits. When pirates come into their port, they have taken to tying a lantern to an old mare's neck and walking her back and forth across the tall sand dunes that litter the coastline. The pirate ships see the light, think it a dock and when they arrive, they run aground! The townsfolk make the *pirates* walk the plank and plunder their cargo."

"And that would be why we are heading for Hatteras Inlet, not Nags Head," a deep baritone voice rumbled from directly behind her.

Oh my word. He is so massive those hands could snap me like a piece of kindling.

Amelia looked about to swoon at the sight of him. With his dark black locks combed into submission and a freshly shaved face, Teache was a ghost of his wild looks. Indeed, compared to his former appearance, the man could almost pass as handsome.

The young girl began to slip down the ladder, losing her balance twice in the first three steps.

"I believe she is seasick. I will go assist her, Captain." Stanzy descended the ladder as quickly as possible. Anything to get out of eyeshot of that piercing black gaze.

Sleep was an unwilling bedfellow. Nightmares, perpetually plagued by the demons of her past life, reared their ugly heads each and every night like a macabre show of paintings, each more hideous than the previous one.

"Where could it be?"

Constanza felt her face flush as she checked the loose floorboard for the third time, hoping she'd some-how missed the stash of money. She only resorted to dipping in the savings when their household exceeded its monthly expenditures.

Lying flat on her stomach, her hand swiped inside the hole to make sure it hadn't been pushed farther in, but not a coin jingled its reply.

She knew immediately where the money had gone—unfortunately she knew nothing about retriev-ing it from a person's veins.

Without pause she stormed into her father's office,

where certificates and awards galore decorated the walls of the erstwhile great man.

The once great man with his face on the desk in a pool of drool.

"Father! Wake up!"

His bleary eyes cracked a slit, but quickly fell shut. They seemed to have a mind of their own. Attempting to rouse him again, Constanza furiously shook his shoulders, which only resulted in his sitting up, whilst his neck lolled grotesquely about. A marionette let loose of his strings, courtesy of liquor.

With no hesitation, she poked him—hard. "You must wake up! We have a grave problem. The apothecary expects payment today, and our money is gone. Do you have money hidden anywhere else?"

He didn't respond.

Her open palm slapped his cheek, leaving an instant welt. Doctor Smythe roused, the anger of the devil burning in his eyes. Constanza felt a rush of air pass her cheek as his first swipe missed. Without time to step back, the second connected with her jawbone. Her father slumped back to his unconscious position as quickly as he'd awakened.

The force of the blow propelled her, cartwheeling her backward. Clutching her cheek, she thought, not for the first time, that she wanted to run. That she had to leave. She couldn't bear this suffering any longer. His beatings and spending all of his days living in the past, while she was expected to continue to live on in the present—alone—wasn't right. She wanted to run away as far as she could and never look back.

As sure as the beating of her heart, she knew she couldn't. Knew she wouldn't.

Trudging up the stairs, muffled sounds issued from behind the nursery door.

Will's crying filled the hallway when she opened the door. Quickly wrapping his tiny body in the fullest blanket she could find, she set out to save them—yet again. She swallowed a threatening sob as she headed outside, balancing Will on her hip.

She fought her way through the blackened snow-filled streets of Bristol.

After what seemed an eternity, they entered the warm pub. Sitting her baby brother on the bar, she dropped her eyes to the floor.

The bartender, an attractive woman in her fortieth year, took one look at the shiner on her cheek. "Not again. What is it this time, love?"

Tears welled in her eyes.

No, I will not cry. If I cry, he wins again and I only bring shame upon myself.

Pressing her lips together, she squared her shoulders and blinked back the tears. "The apothecary needs payment, or we will only have the medicines from the herb garden. Unfortunately, last year was not a productive crop and my supplies are low."

"All right then. Take William upstairs, love."

After complying, Constanza re-entered the bar and drew an apron tightly around her slim body, then picked up the first night's round of drinks. If she worked 'til closing, she should have enough to get through—this time.

Eyes fluttering open to the day, Constanza smiled. As far as she could cipher, this grand morning was day one hundred and twenty, and land—beautiful dry unmoving land—should be within sight in the next twenty-four hours. The three of them had made it through their ordeal alive, albeit each was a good fifteen pounds lighter.

Katrina of course was the most distressed. "Constanza? How will I ever land a husband with a body so frail? Why, I look like you!"

Will's eyes were shadowed with dark half moons below them, which she knew to be a mineral deficiency of some sort. She was only able to bring a few of her medical books aboard as they had barely enough for the reduced passage on what she'd surmised to be a rumrunner.

A small hole had been chewed in one of the hold's

barrels by Teredo worms. The ship must have been in tropical climates prior to this voyage by her estimation. Tropical water weeds were still being removed from the ship's hull, and the mollusks, or pileworms, had not only burrowed into some of the barrels of the precious rum, but into the ship's wooden hull as well. Their tube like shell structures could be seen outside as long as six feet in some places. She'd spied them while hanging her head over the side during the first two weeks. Vomiting into the sea had become her favorite way to pass the time. From years spent with her uncle, she knew the worms could actually compromise the stability of a ship.

Wouldn't that be just grand if, during the last days of the voyage, the ship sprung a leak and sent us to the bottom for naught?

She suppressed a bitter smile. On this subject she uttered a word to no one.

Before their departure, she'd given her books to her uncle and had decided she would write to him and have them sent when funds and circumstances permitted.

A loud bang rent the air. Musket fire? All about the cabin, tired heads lifted in response to the unusual early morning sound.

Boom! The entire hull shook with the vibration.

Constanza saw Will place a protective arm about Katrina's shoulders, as she filed in with the queue of men headed topside to investigate the disturbance.

The men's upturned faces were drenched by a deluge streaming from the topside hole. A storm, a *squall* raged in the sky above. Pushing her way through the sodden crowd, she saw sailors quickly battening down hatches and preparing for the storm. The captain ferociously barked orders right and left, his huge frame working at steering the craft.

Constanza lurched as the boat's starboard side raised high on a wave. All men topside plummeted to the deck. An ear-splitting crack occurred as the vessel ran aground. Massive swells, sheer walls of water, pummeled the deck. Every man tied himself to the rigging. She wondered if this were a hurricane.

"The Diamond Shoals, Captain! We are done for!" yelled one crewmember.

"You directionless fool!" Teache screamed at his first mate. The captain's hand strayed to his pistol, but then his gaze met Stanzy's and he replaced it on the wheel.

She squinted and shielded her eyes to ward off the driving rain, trying to assess how far from shore the vessel had lodged itself.

Who is that? Or what is that?

A lone figure stood on the sands of what was presumably the Hatteras coastline waving his arms. He beckoned them eerily to the shore. Jack, the Sheep dog, bounded from below deck as if hearing a dog whistle and began to run back and forth beside the rail. The first mate came over and tied a rope to Jack's neck and pitched the dog into the roaring waves.

Stanzy screamed, "What are you doing?" She was soon joined by a wailing Will who'd just witnessed his dog chucked overboard.

"Miss, it may be our only chance. Me last squall, a horse was thrown over and took the rope to shore, and we were able to make it through the waves."

Constanza crawled up onto the deck. "No, Will, stay down there!"

Katrina appeared as hands pulling her brother out of sight and back into the hull's topside hole.

Constanza struggled with the wet knot as she tethered herself to the rigging. She held her breath as she watched the Sheep dog's progress through the Atlantic water. His furry ears dipped below the waves and reappeared too many times for her to count. All the while, the stranger at the shore kept beckoning.

After what seemed like years, the dog reached the shore, and the man placed the rope around a huge tree.

"Get rid of the cargo!" yelled the first mate. He entered the hull, adding, "If ye want to live, do as I say!"

~ *Chapter Two* ~

Passengers lined up on the ladder and underneath in the hull, waiting to take the plunge into the Atlantic water.

"Will, Kitty, come to me!" Constanza screamed over the howling wind. They hurried to her side. "Kitty, go first, I will watch you and keep Will with me." Taking a rope, she tied Will to her torso.

Kitty slowly ascended down the rope. The ship lunged toward the water, nearly on its side, plunging her into the water.

Constanza tried to push her uncle's voice from her head which echoed the sailor's nickname for the sea off the barrier islands—*The Graveyard of the Atlantic.*

"Don't let go!" Constanza screamed into the gale. She began her own descent and felt Will struggling behind her. "Pray, Will," she yelled over the cacophonous combination of wind, water, and wailing passengers.

She felt rather than heard him mumble, until waves hit and forced them under. Wave after wave pushed them beneath the salty water. Desperately clutching the rope with both hands, she inched her way toward the shore. Fear surged through her as she realized something was in front of her. Tentatively reaching out, she felt her sister's hair.

Stanzy gently shoved Kitty to indicate her presence behind her on the rope. "We are going to make it," she muttered optimistically. *I have to keep them safe. Please, God, do not let them die. I am responsible—for them—for all of this. Please, not here. Do not let us die under the waves.*

A wall of water crashed down on them, sending them surging to the sandy floor. They had reached the breakers. With every ounce of remaining strength, Stanzy kicked and swam toward the surface. Then she watched with joy as Katrina fought past the breakers.

Will was still tied to Constanza's back, but even with her excellent physical strength, she knew the battle was futile. She gasped for air moments before another swell hit. She knew Will wouldn't be able to hold on much longer, his eleven-year-old lungs not strong enough.

Miraculously, sand scraped against the side of her face as she hit the sandbar. Sand! *We are close to shore. I must get to the top of the water.* She forced her legs beneath her and flailed for the bottom, for somewhere to stand.

Unsure of what she was feeling next, she realized hands were pulling her up—up to the water's surface. They breached the surface and gasped for air; she couldn't see her rescuer. When she glanced to the right, she saw many men in the surf, fishing humans out from under the waves. All the while, the storm raged. Water fell in diagonal sheets across the white tipped waves.

Oh thank you. Thank you.

Jack stood on the shore, cowering under a tree, loyally awaiting his master. Blackness closed her vision to a pinprick...then all went quiet.

The smell of bread baking permeated her senses. For a moment she was disoriented. Mama baked bread almost every morning, but Mama was long gone. Stanzy bolted stark upright, her eyes searching as she assessed her surroundings. Vaulting out of bed—the world swooned like a night spent drinking. Vertigo smacked her in the head, the room undulating around her. She collapsed to her knees, disgorging seawater all over the floor.

On all fours, she crawled away from the remnants of her last meal, forcing herself across the room. Another bed was barely visible in the moonlight. Struggling to a stand, she peered over its side. In the dim candlelight, she made out the forms of her brother and sister.

We are all alive, but where are we? How did we get here?

Silently slumping to the floor, her face in her hands, she muffled uncontrollable sobs. Not often did she permit herself the luxury of crying. At an early age she'd learned that weeping in her household was a useless emotion, and never made any of her problems disappear. Ever since Mama died eleven years ago at the time of Will's birth, Stanzy, at sixteen, had started living the life of an adult. Katrina and Will's reliance on her used to frighten her. But now she had little time to worry, her daily thoughts consumed with the responsibility of trying to keep all of them alive and out of harm's way.

Tears stung her sand chafed cheeks like acid. Once she opened the floodgates, it became almost impossible to halt. All the closed Pandora's boxes of her mind, filled with hateful memories, sprung open. Her mama had once said, 'Once the door to a closed soul is opened, it is not easily shut.' *How right she was!*

Mama, why did you have to leave me to care for them alone? I do not think I can live one more day in this soul. We are destitute, and I don't know if I will even be able to feed them tonight. What was I thinking...to leave all I have known behind? I do not know the land, the customs, or where to begin. I am not strong enough to bear this much longer.

For just a moment, she allowed herself the luxury of imagining what it would be like to have someone hold *her* and tell her everything would be all right. She hadn't been comforted in such a way since the age of sixteen.

A low moan arose from the bed as Will thrashed against the blankets wrapped about him. A small column of light shone across the bed. Framed in the doorway, a man was in silhouette. At five feet nine inches, Stanzy was considered tall for a woman, and she guessed the stranger to be about six feet.

His voice whispered into the darkness, "Miss Smythe, are you all right?"

Startled, she responded, "How do you know my name?"

"Come out here, let the others sleep. Especially the boy, he was almost overcome." His shadowy hand beckoned to her in the darkness.

She walked toward him into the faint candlelight. She stopped in her tracks dumbfounded.

He is beautiful.

The man's hair and eyes were dark and somber, his face housed a small half moon scar by the corner of his mouth.

Is he blushing because I am staring at him? Stop staring! I am an imbecile!

One hand fidgeted, twirling his hat round and round. The other he thrust out. "I am Lucian Blackwell. I was sent to Hattaras by my employer to collect you and your family to bring you all back to StoneWater."

"Oh, I see." A raucous laugh shifted her staring at the man. Looking down over a banister, she deduced the accommodations to be a pub. Morning patrons shuffled about, intent on breakfast.

"As you surmised, I am Constanza Smythe, and in the bed are my sister, Katrina, and my brother, William. I am the one who has been hired to be the governess to the Hopkins' children."

"Yea, I figured you were the governess as you are the older one..." He blushed scarlet, apparently realizing too late the faux pas. He added hastily, "I mean older is fine. I am older..." With that final pronouncement, he turned a shade of puce she'd never witnessed in all of her days.

"Pa!" called a boy from behind the man. "Is the boy around yet?"

Lucian held up a hand to quiet the lad. "That's my boy. His name is Benjamin. Ever since he heard you were arriving he has been very anxious to meet your brother. StoneWater has few boys and many girls, so he insisted I bring him despite the 'cane. Besides, I was born and raised here; we Bankers see canes each and every year."

Constanza smiled at him.

26

His countenance is so open. I wonder if he is always this way. Not that I care—the child sitting at the bar is proof he is not available. Even if I were interested—which I am not.

"Who pulled me from the water?" she asked, trying not to think about his handsome appearance; trying to ignore how close he stood and how wonderful he smelled—a decidedly masculine scent of soap and leather.

"I did." He smiled and it took her breath away. "I saw you with the boy tied to your back, so I knew you would not last long in that surf. The swells must have been fifteen feet. You were very brave to come here with them in tow."

"Not too brave, but practical. We do what we must to get along."

"The doctor will be here soon to check on them, but earlier he stopped by and said your family would make a full recovery."

"Yes, I looked at them myself."

He raised an eyebrow in silent question.

"My father was a physician, and I assisted him for many years before his death. Also my mother was a midwife and healer, so I know a bit about it."

"Mr. Hopkins did choose well then, to have a dual governess and healer." He led her down the stairs to the bar room. "He will well get his money's worth."

She thought she detected a note of sarcasm in his last words, but he didn't speak again.

What he did next confused her. Lucian placed a hand on the small of her back and led her through the crowd. As he did, she felt his hand tremble.

The carriage rattled its way along twisting dirt roads, leading them away from the ocean's edge into the Pamlico Sound area.

Will virtually risked death—his head hung so far out of the carriage window in a vain attempt to drink in every piece of scenery.

"Stanzy, look at those bogs!" His voice barely

discernible on the inside of the carriage. "Do you know what kind of animals they have at the plantation? Do you think it will be all right if Jack sleeps in my room? How many boys are there?"

Constanza yelled, doubting he could hear her, "Will! I have no idea how to answer any of those questions, except there are two boys I know of—Mr. Hopkins' boy, Lucas, and the farm manager's boy, Benjamin Blackwell."

"Yes, Mr. Blackwell is *very* easy on the eyes!" This from Katrina, who was busy wrapping her dark brown ringlets around her fingers attempting to curl them into submission. "This air makes my hair straight. I thought once we were off that floating death trap the air would improve. Only Mr. Teache made the trip tolerable."

"Katrina. Katrina, pay attention! I realize he was attracted to you, but let us try to set our sights higher than the likes of Mr. Teache."

"Oh, do be honest. Before things went awry, I saw you examining his fine male anatomy on a number of occasions."

"Well, in a barbaric sort of way, he is attractive— very tall and muscular, but I am afraid I will need more than that to hold my interest."

"Oh, you are so tiresome," Katrina retorted and resumed staring out the window.

They were silent when the carriage turned the corner onto the path to StoneWater and an imposing manor came into view. It was one of the largest manor's the three had ever seen. The estate proper sat on a raised area, evidently by design in case of flooding, and slave quarters, barns and liveries were situated about the property.

"Will, you must sit still and behave. I have no concept of how staunch the Hopkinses may be in their puritan ideals, so we must not offend them. We have spoken before of the rules and expectations in a puritan house."

"Yes, I know. Not too much running about or playing, no yelling or screaming..."

"Or acting too happy or sad, for that matter," chimed in Katrina, never removing her eyes from the manor. "Oh, sister, perhaps this long journey will have been worth the risk after all."

"Do not be too hasty—we have not even met my employers as yet."

The carriage rumbled to a stop in front of the manor and within moments several slaves rushed forward to assist with their meager belongings.

Lucian appeared and opened the door. His hand rose to grasp hers, steadying her down the stairs. He held it a few seconds too long. As she slid it away, his thumb traced a line down her palm, sending shivers up her spine.

The door of the manor opened and a man boldly strode across the porch. Stanzy assumed this was her employer, Mr. Hopkins.

She curtsied and said, "I am—"

"Yes, you must be Constanza. I'm Mr. Hopkins. I have had many a correspondence with your fine uncle, Channing. He has already written to inquire as to your arrival."

"This is my sister, Katrina, and my brother, Will."

Constanza noticed Mr. Hopkins' eyes slid immediately to Kitty's ample curves, until he heard the slam of a door and averted his gaze.

"Welcome to StoneWater." The lady of the manor was very plain—there was no other way to describe her. She made the most of her features, however, and her face virtually shone with a well-scrubbed complexion. To offset her lack of beauty, she dressed in the latest fashion from Paris, which Constanza was sure Kitty had noticed.

"It is a pleasure to meet each of you. And yes, Lucas will be very glad to have another lad to conspire with," Hopkins said, rocking back and forth on his heels. The man stole a glance at Katrina whenever it appeared Mrs. Hopkins wasn't looking. "Blackwell, my good man, could you show Will and Ben where Lucas has got to? I am afraid he has run amok since our last governess departed."

"Yes, sir."

Constanza led him to William's bags in the back of the carriage. Lucian abruptly grabbed her elbow, and leaned so close she felt his lips graze her earlobe. He whispered, "If you need anything, day or night, while you are here, my cabin is not far from the wing in which you are housed. Just call and I will be there in a moment's notice."

Drawing back to regard him, dark, serious eyes returned her gaze. He gave her a quick nod and headed toward the boys. Chills crept down her spine at his words. *Why in the world would I need him?*

Stanzy watched him walk toward the right wing of the manor, flanked by Will and one of the servant's boys. She couldn't help but notice his perfectly proportioned body.

He is beautiful. And he is married. If he is even entertaining the idea of bedding me, then I know full well to run away from him!

"Constanza?" Mr. Hopkins' voice brought her back to reality. "My name is Ian, and this is my wife, Sarah. The maid will show you to your quarters. We will begin tomorrow with your expected responsibilities regarding the training of our children."

As they wound their way up the back servants' staircase, she physically felt her sister quaking with anticipation. Katrina had always been influenced by wealth and power; this whole experience had to be a paradise for her.

They entered the three adjoining rooms and the maid departed. Katrina launched herself into the air and bounced on the four poster bed. "Can you believe it? We have *never* had a room to ourselves. This is going to be wonderful."

"Katrina, now would be a good time to discuss how *you* plan to earn your keep here at the plantation. Having finished your schooling with me, you would make a good teaching assistant. There are at least the three students, and perhaps we might teach some of the slaves' children as well—"

"Are you mad? Mr. Hopkins is a gentleman, and will not want his son learning side by side with his servants' children. Why that is disgraceful!"

Constanza shook her head slowly and inhaled a deep breath before facing her sister. "You know, you are so much like our father with your class ideals. I believe, and so did Mother, that all people are equal in the eyes of God regardless of color or social status."

"Stop with your ideals! You will not change the world."

Stanzy sighed and went over to look out the window for Will. This was a frequent old argument that would probably go on forever, if she permitted it. She recalled one of her uncle's favorite sayings: 'You cannot argue with an idiot, without looking like one yourself.'

The rap on the door made them both start as their raw, tightly wound nerves had had enough excitement after battling the Atlantic surf.

Katrina strode to the door, opened it, and gave Lucian what Stanzy recognized as her most seductive pose. Her hand settled on her hip, her head tilted coquettishly to one side, chest thrust forward—of course.

"All right, Will?" she asked as her brother pushed in.

"Yeah, better than all right! I met Ben and Lucas and they are going to teach me about the horses and their tack and..."

Constanza pulled him to her in a tight hug and said, "Thank you, Mr. Blackwell."

"Call me Lucian."

Katrina replied, "Thank you, Lucian." She shut the door with a click.

The windowpanes shook as thunder rumbled close by. Constanza rolled over and smiled into the darkness; Will had stolen into her bed sometime after the storm had begun. Finally he had a room of his own, but old habits die hard.

The dog was also now at the bottom of her bed. She

felt him trembling at her feet, fearful of the thunder and lightning.

She moved closer to Will and buried her face into the top of his head, breathing deeply his scent, which had almost lost its baby smell. That's when she heard it. The calm melted away as quickly as it had arrived.

What was that?

Birds screaming?

Bats?

All was quiet again.

Then upstairs, straight above her room, she heard it. Full force screams and the sound of a heavy object repeatedly striking the wooden floor directly above her bed.

Bang! Bang! Bang!

She slipped out of bed and padded over to the window. Across the yard, Lucian ran through the storm, a lantern swinging from his arm. She watched him approach and disappear below her window. He must have entered the service entrance into the kitchen.

Bang! Bang! Bang!

More screams. Startled, she jumped backward as something hurtled past her window from above and sailed through the night sky to the wet ground below. She peered through the darkness, but was unable to make out the object lying in the rain.

Heavy booted feet clambered up the stairs and past her room. Running to her door, she cracked it in time to see Lucian hurrying up the stairwell, his clothes dripping water in his path. When he disappeared on the landing above she heard a door right above her head open, then close. Quietly, she pressed her door shut.

She tiptoed to the rocker and sat, bringing her legs to her chest and straining her ears to hear. The banging and screaming ceased.

Constanza sat a long time, trying to hear Lucian's retreat down the stairs, but sleep claimed her and she never heard him leave.

"Stanzy, are you awake?"

She opened her eyes to Katrina shaking her, pulling her away from a bizarre dream world, where screams and wind all mingled together into a cacophony of sound.

"What time is it?"

"It is darn near nine o'clock! And you still in bed!"

"I must have overslept. Where is Will?"

"Lucian came to collect him at about 6:30. But who cares about that? I hear visitors downstairs, and I wanted you to help me pin my hair up."

Katrina's cheeks glowed and her neck flushed clear down to her low cut gown, where her breasts formed two perfect mounds of flesh. Constanza pushed the covers aside and glanced at her own upper body, which reminded her of an adolescent boy.

"Who is it?" Stanzy asked, as she climbed from bed and began to dress.

"I do not know, but I saw several gentlemen arrive in a carriage."

They made their way down the formal staircase into the foyer. Several men could be seen through the slightly open sitting-room door.

Stanzy stopped dead in her tracks. *Edward Teache. What is he doing here?*

Evidently having heard them approach, Mr. Hopkins turned and strode toward the open door, with Teache following behind.

"Ah...Mr. Teache, might I present my new governess, Constanza, and her sister, Katrina?" Hopkins said with a most flamboyant bow.

"I have already made their acquaintance, Ian. After all, it was on my ship they arrived in the Banks. Perhaps you were not aware as it is a new ship called *Freedom*. Not the one I previously had in my employ."

"I see. Well, if you would excuse us ladies, we have business to attend. Constanza, I will meet with you in two hours to discuss plans for my daughter's education."

Stanzy left the men to their business, and she and

33

Katrina entered the servants' kitchen. Seated at the table were an elderly black man and Lucian. A heavyset woman stirred a pot at the stove. Without turning around, she asked, "Lucian, you need more coffee?"

He cradled a mug in his hands, steam rising into his face. Dark black circles shadowed his eyes, and he vigorously rubbed a hand over his face.

"No, Bess, I still have plenty."

The silence was awkward, then Lucian and Constanza both fixed their eyes on something floating through the air in the kitchen. It was a ladybug.

Constanza looked down the table and saw Lucian smiling into his mug. "Did I miss something?"

He shook his head, still smiling.

Introductions were made, and before she knew it she was headed for the barn on Lucian's arm, having accepted his offer to give her a tour of the plantation.

Why has he wrapped my arm in his? What is he playing at? He smells so good I cannot stand it. I do not think I will hear a word he says to me. I sound like an idiotic school girl!

Lucian stopped and stared at her. Apparently he'd asked her a question.

When she merely stared, he spoke again. "The main crop is tobacco, for which I am responsible, besides my job overseeing the slaves. The small quarters behind the manor is a schoolhouse. Would you like to walk over and see it?"

"Yes, thank you." She wrestled to keep her words in check, wanting to pummel him with questions about the previous night. If she had Lucian figured right, he was the calculating, silent type, who only spoke after careful consideration. If she wanted answers, she would have to play her cards right.

When he opened the door she sucked in her breath as she entered a beautifully designed and decorated cottage. Small desks were aligned in front of a larger desk for her use. A few seemingly misplaced items lay about, such as ropes, and of course, the standard switch. But one sight made her look twice—a chain attached to one of the walls.

She could only surmise that maybe animals were once housed here, before they made it into the schoolhouse.

"This is wonderful. I am sure I will be able to accomplish much with the children. Lucian, is your boy to attend as well?"

He nodded. "Yes. I have an arrangement with Mr. Hopkins. Guess you could say he inherited me with the farm. Mrs. Hopkins' father, Mr. Kirkaldy, used to own it before he passed on. When Sarah married Ian Hopkins, her father gave him several conditions he had to fulfill in order to gain possession of the plantation. My request that Ben be educated was one of them. Mr. Kirkaldy had only daughters, no male heirs."

"I see. How old is Ben?"

"He is nine years out."

Here I go. Best to call him on it now.

She looked him dead in the eye and said, "His mother must be thrilled that he will have an education as well."

"His mother is dead. She died of smallpox when Ben was three years old."

Constanza felt the blood drain from her face and surmised she was as white as the cotton bobbing outside on the breeze. She reached over and placed her hand on his. "I am so sorry, I had no idea. I lost both my parents and have been caring for my brother and sister since I was sixteen. You have done a wonderful job. Ben seems very happy."

"He is a blessing, one of the few I have had." He turned away from her, checking the sky. "We had better head back to the manor as it is almost time for you to meet with Hopkins."

As they walked to the manor, Stanzy kept stealing glances at him from out of the corner of her eye. *My word he is dark and beautiful. I cannot believe I am acting this way. I detest silly women who act this way...*

Although she waited into the evening for the

summons to see Mr. Hopkins, it never transpired. She also wanted desperately to inquire of the chains in the schoolhouse, but decided to wait for a more opportune time. One thing for certain, she didn't want to offend her new employer.

Constanza's eyes popped open from a deep sleep.

There it was again—*screams from upstairs.*

She sat up in bed, and guessed it was about four in the morning.

Bang! Bang!

Fully awake, she kicked off her covers and rushed to the window. Sure enough, throwing his overcoat over his bare chest, Lucian bolted through the swirling wind toward the house again. Throwing open the window and thrusting her head out, she craned her neck to see the floor above. The only thing she could see was a flickering light, most likely from a lantern inside the room.

Constanza padded to the door and with her ear to the wood listened for Lucian's footsteps. It wasn't a long wait; she heard him as he hurriedly climbed the stairs. He passed her door on the way to the steps to the third floor.

Enough of this nonsense, she thought. She flung the door open and hastened quickly behind him on the steps. As his forearm raised to knock, she took hold of it, causing him to startle.

"Lucian, what is going on? Who is making all that noise? Is someone hurt? I told you I have been trained as a healer, let me help."

"He did not tell you, did he? The bloody coward. Well, this is not how I would have told you, Constanza, but come. Meet your other pupil."

~ *Chapter Three* ~

Lucian's eyes welled with tears. The care-worn expression on his face led her to believe he'd been dealing with whatever was behind the door for a very long time.

Stanzy's stomach lurched in response to a gruesome sight. In the middle of the room was a tiny girl, probably no more than five. Bright dark eyes met hers and locked. Long brown locks tumbled down her tiny back in waves. However, on closer inspection, large matted clumps interwove throughout the curls. Only the fur of alley cats back in Bristol could compete with these malignant tangles.

The child's back extended to extreme as a scream as shrill as any banshee escaped her lips. Thrashing forward, her head gave a sickening crunch on the desk in front of her. When she raised it, an angry red welt rose to a lump on her forehead. Tied onto a chair, the girl stopped flailing momentarily to look at who had entered the room. Ropes restrained her torso to the chair, which now rocked violently, threatening to tip with each flagellation of her tautly wound body.

Her head rocked purposefully toward Bess, who knelt beside her. Eyes blazed with hatred at her own miscalculation as Bess moved out of the way of the head butting. Walloping her head on the back of the chair, her eyes grew dimmer with each successful blow.

Whap! Whap!

"Oh, my." Constanza rushed to the girl's side and attempted to restrain the wild child, to no avail. The tiny body gave another great arch as she struck the final blow. Blood poured from the back of her scalp, drowning curls and clumps of hair alike.

Bess emitted a low, keening cry, removed the child's restraints and held a wet cloth to the back of her head. Gently lifting her from the chair, the girl seemed to disappear in the old woman's embrace.

"I will put her to bed, Miss. She will be all right now. You come back tomorrow, and me and you—we have a good talk about this little one."

Turning, Constanza locked eyes with Lucian, his hand partially covering his face. She caught sight of the track of a single tear before he wiped it away, "She is very sick, Stanzy."

Constanza followed him down the stairs and into the kitchen. She set coffee to boil. Soon the aromatic scent of the fresh brew permeated the kitchen. Constanza filled and handed Lucian a steaming mug, then sat beside him. "Please, Lucian, tell me everything." The sun would be rising soon and with it all of their responsibilities.

Lucian dragged a rough hand across his face. He heaved a sigh. "She has been this way since she was about one year out. Sometimes, she is like an animal—biting, kicking, spitting. When that queerness takes her, she will try to hurt you if she gets the chance. When she was almost two, things got even worse. That was when her mother and father quit going upstairs to see her anymore."

"They what?"

"Yeah. They have not seen her in over three years. The Hopkinses are people with little patience for regular folk, let alone sick ones. They have set Bess to care for her, and a long string of governesses, I'm afraid."

Constanza nodded, the pieces of the puzzle fitting together in her mind. "No wonder they permitted me to bring my brother and sister; they were desperate."

"Yes, I imagine they were. Most folks round here know about her, so I reckon that is why they needed to write to England to find you."

"Are you related to her, Lucian? I see you going up there each time she is in a rage."

"No, but I cannot bear to think of her alone with only Bess, who God knows loves and cares for her the best she can. But she knows me, and when she has a good day, she has even let me hold her, but it doesn't last. She cannot talk and she cannot control herself."

"All right. I will need to be close to her to assess how deep the damage runs within her. And I swear I will try and do my best to improve her life. The first thing we need to do is get her out of that room."

"I do take her sometimes, but I have to be careful. She tries to run away, and she is very strong as you saw. She has no comprehension of danger. Her parents do not know that I take her out of her prison, so I am trusting you not to divulge my secret. When I saw you out in the sea being almost mommicked to death, I somehow knew you were a different type of woman."

"Many men find me too boyish," she said flatly.

Her hands were sitting on the table in plain sight. Without a second glance, he chose to take her left hand, the one with the deformity.

"I like a woman who thinks for herself." His gaze was unblinking. "Thank you. I could really use some help with the child. Her name is Megan."

Constanza stared down at the servants' table that evening, lost in thought. It had been a long day, since they'd been up before dawn. She couldn't understand the happy disposition of all those gathered. Vaguely, she heard talk of rumrunners in the area and pirates sabotaging merchant ships on their way into the outer banks of the state. She smiled as Kitty and Will sat, unmoving, entranced at Alfonse's news of the pirates from his visit to Bath. Pirates had infiltrated the peace-loving villages and smuggled rum into the area. But all these rumors seemed mindless and silly tonight. All *she* could think of was the scene she'd witnessed earlier.

Megan.

In all my years of assisting with amputees, plague and influenza, I never saw anything that resembles what afflicts her. What is it? A brain fever? I always know, but I do not know this.

From down the table, Lucian sat also uninvolved in the conversation. He merely stared, his deep brown eyes fixated on her, his fingers interlaced before his mouth. If she didn't know his kind disposition, the intensity of his stare might frighten her. She fidgeted in her chair.

I have never had a man look at me like he does. His eyes follow my every move. And yet he does not speak. I long to know what is in his head.

Lucian's eyes never left her until the servants began to depart from the table.

Constanza walked out to the pizzer, as these people called their porch, and sat on the swing.

The clomp of Lucian's approaching bootfalls sent chills rippling up her back. He placed his hand on her shoulder. "Mebbe we should move your quarters. I sincerely doubt you will get any rest below Meg's room."

She guessed many would see the touches he bestowed on her as inappropriate, but she didn't care.

All I can hear is my heart beating in my ears when he touches me.

Indeed, she found herself longing for him to touch her more. It seemed he took every opportunity he could to graze her hand, or the small of her back. Many times she thought she felt his hand trembling. Like her own legs.

Dropping her head back to look up at him, she said, "I would need to discuss that with Mr. and Mrs. Hopkins. It has been two weeks and they have not mentioned Megan to me as yet. They have only spoken of their expectations for Lucas."

As he laced his fingers into her hair, she licked her dry lips and felt as if she might swoon. She swallowed hard before she continued. "I intend on dealing with it tomorrow. Why were you smiling in the kitchen this morning?"

His lips turned up and he hung his head. She was certain, if there were more light, she would have been able to see red on his cheeks again.

"There is a tale that says when two people see a

ladybug at the same time, they are destined to be together."

"Really?"

"Really..."

She felt remorse as his fingers disengaged from her hair. The interlude was lost in the noise of the gaggle of boys that had made their way onto the porch.

"I have heard rumors, Constanza, that you have already made Megan's acquaintance."

Ian Hopkins' slight frame and billowy white shirt usually made his appearance quite harmless. But today, pale blue eyes beneath his furrowed brow were barely perceptible from where he stood behind his massive desk.

"Yes, sir. I have only seen her one time so far. I apologize for not telling you. It was purely by accident. As I am certain you know, my room is directly below hers, and she is up most nights 'til sunrise, so I couldn't help, but—"

"Yes, she is quite mad, I am afraid. A hopeless case. We are still trying to determine whether she is possessed or insane. I assure you that she has the very best physician and clergyman available. What I expect of you, is to try to make her more civilized, if possible. I would expect you to conduct private sessions in her room. She requires lessons in proper behavior, which come naturally to a normal child, such as learning to sit at a table to eat, how to use utensils. By the last report, I heard she still uses her hands to feed herself, and throws her fork and spoon with deadly accuracy."

You pompous dandy!

Stanzy's insides quivered with rage and she swallowed the bile in her mouth. Pain shot through her hands as her fingernails dug into her palms. She struggled to master her rage and the chastisement that threatened to spill from her lips.

"I do not believe she is insane or possessed, sir. I believe she is *ill*. I have been trained as a healer and a physician's helper, as you know from my Uncle Delvin's letters. I will do my best to do all for Megan that I can."

Hopkins winced at the sound of her name, which Stanzy had never heard him utter. He referred to her only as *my daughter.* "Yes, very well. You are to meet with me monthly and discuss how my son's lessons are progressing as we have discussed—math, French, writing and reading."

After their meeting, Constanza walked outside and inhaled deeply of the morning air in an attempt to calm herself. She stomped down to the area she'd begun to clear for her herb garden. Kneeling, she began mentally planning the rows for each plant. Lost in thought, she startled when she heard a low, male voice.

"Constanza, darlin', I never figured you for a farmer. You seemed much more at home on me sloop than with your hands buried in the dirt."

Her head shot upright, knocking her off balance. She bit her lip as her bottom hit the ground.

Edward Teache towered over her, his massive frame completely blotting out the sun. She shivered in his shadow. Power seemed to emanate from his person.

"Good day, Mr. Teache. Here for business again?" She struggled to keep her voice from cracking.

Look him in the eye. Do not let him know he frightens you.

"Aye, call me Edward, Miss. Hadn't we already spent an entire voyage across the seas together? Surely for a man and a woman, that means somethin'?"

There is something odd about his eyes. Something... dead.

"All right, Edward it is, then." Her mind replayed the sounds of musket fire ringing in her ears. Women's muffled cries from up on deck flitted in and out of her consciousness. This wasn't a man to be trifled with, and she was no fool.

"Would you care to take a turn with me then? Or better yet, how about a ride to Beaufort, to me new home? 'Tis called Hammock House, and is along a beautiful creek—Taylor Creek. I have been thinking it is time I settle down. Been out to sea all me life. So what do you say? Is a ride to Beaufort in order then?" He extended his huge hand to help her up out of the mud.

"I am sorry, but that will not be possible, sir. You see, Miss Smythe is expected to begin the children's lessons in less than an hour." From out of nowhere Lucian appeared, his face pinched in an expression she hadn't seen in him before—anger.

Teache, at six four, was taller than Lucian's six foot frame. Lucian's face muscles were taut with determination.

"Blackwell." Teache spoke his name as a curse word. "I was not aware you are Constanza's employer. Perhaps I will go and see if Hopkins might part with his governess for a few days?"

"You do that." Lucian abruptly grabbed Stanzy's hand, yanked her to a standing position, and half dragged her in the direction of the schoolhouse.

Once they were out of Teache's sight, he jerked her roughly to him and spoke with some urgency. "Stanzy, he is a very dangerous man. Do not be fooled by his charms, he—"

She touched her finger to his lips to quiet him, then placed her mouth to his, silencing him completely. Never in her life had she pushed herself on a man, but she couldn't seem to help doing so with this one. His quiet and sincere ways were foreign and too incredibly appealing to her. He kissed her back with such passion, he frightened her.

When their lips parted, his forehead rested against hers for a moment. He didn't speak.

"I am not fooled by Edward Teache, Lucian. Nor am I interested in any sort of a man such as he. I prefer a true character to one of bravado and show." She smiled, her eyes focusing on something beyond him.

"What?" he said quietly.

"I beg you, look there."

He followed her pointing finger. Behind him, a wall teemed with movement. Thousands of ladybugs crawled and flew on and around the window sill.

"I will go 'round up the lads for you," he said and

turned to walk away from her. Then he glanced at her over his shoulder and awarded her with a smile that permeated his entire face. The brittle enclosure surrounding her heart shattered in a million pieces.

I am sure I have never met a man like him in all of my days. 'Tis over for me. I will never be satisfied with anyone but him.

After the daily lessons were finished, she ambled into the manor's entryway in time to catch the tail end of a spirited conversation.

"Oh yes, Ian. It would be marvelous to have another woman along on our trip to Beaufort and Bath."

Katrina was standing next to Mrs. Hopkins, positively shaking with delight. "Oh, Stanzy!" her sister called when she caught sight of her. "Mr. and Mrs. Hopkins have asked me to go on their trip into the towns? You will not mind if I go, will you?"

The man of the manor stood, rocking back and forth with self-importance on his high-heeled boots. He turned to fix his collar in the mirror. Constanza was reminded of a peacock pruning its feathers.

"Mr. Hopkins, are you sure Katrina will not be any trouble?"

"No, no. I daresay she will keep Mrs. Hopkins well occupied. When she travels with me on business, she finds it very dull indeed."

With their common interests in the latest fashion trends from abroad, Katrina and Mrs. Hopkins had become fast friends. Neither had the slightest interest in plantation life. Even Ian Hopkins seemed to take every possible opportunity to travel to the larger towns. Stanzy wondered if he had any idea what was occurring in his fields, at any time. Or even what *crops* he grew.

"If you are certain, it will be all right, then," she said, still unconvinced this trip would end well. Her high-strung greyhound of a sister wasn't easily leashed.

"I have to go gather my bags!" Katrina flew up the stairs, petticoats and frills trailing behind her.

Oh my word. She is so impetuous. At least that is a

constant.

"Please watch her carefully, Mr. Hopkins. Katrina is a bit...careless."

Megan sat cross-legged in the corner of her room, her eyes closed. Her room was elegantly furnished with a four-poster canopy bed and polished hardwood floors. Dolls were strewn about everywhere.

"A perfect prison," whispered Constanza.

Signs of mental instability were evident everywhere. Most dolls' faces had been chewed off or broken; chairs with ropes on them accompanied each table. A single tiny chair with ropes sat facing the window. Stanzy swallowed hard, staring at the solitary chair, as if it personified this solitary little girl.

Several items she'd never seen before were strewn about. Large pins and many sharp metal objects were housed on a shelf far above Megan's reach. But for all the room's elegance, noticeably absent was a lack of decoration, presumably because Bess realized Megan would break objects or use them as weapons on herself or other unsuspecting persons.

On her hands and knees, Stanzy crawled toward Megan who sat hunched in the corner. The girl put her hands over her eyes and tried to bury her face into her legs.

When she got to within five feet of her, Megan began to growl. Deep guttural vibrations echoed in the quiet room. But Stanzy wasn't frightened; in fact, the noises sounded so forlorn to her that she was motivated to keep crawling.

From the other room, she heard Bess whisper, "She not too smart is she?"

She picked a doll up from the floor and said, "Hello, Meg. I am Stanzy."

Without warning, Megan vaulted onto Stanzy's chest, knocking her to the floor. Her tiny fingers ripped at Stanzy's face like talons. The girl's fingernails were so long, they curled over the tips of her fingers.

Bess opened the door, but Stanzy screamed, "I am

fine. Leave us."

Stanzy flipped Meg off and rolled, pinning her little arms. She whispered into her ear, "I know you understand me. You are just a little girl—a scared, angry little girl."

Megan's little body slumped, her struggling faded to whimpers.

"I am going to let you go, but you cannot scratch me again, do you understand?"

Releasing her, the child curled into an unmoving ball, her eyes squeezed tightly shut. Constanza stood and went around the room closing all the drapes. She began to light candles, high up, so Megan couldn't reach them.

After a time, Meg finally opened her eyes and really looked at her for the first time.

Stanzy stood by the drapes, and she split them slightly to let a sliver of light into the dark bed chamber. Meg howled in pain and covered her eyes.

"She is photophobic!" Stanzy cried triumphantly.

"What are you talking about?" came the muffled reply from behind the adjacent door.

Stanzy stuck her head in and said to Bess, "From now on, 'til I tell you otherwise, the only light in Meg's room is to be candlelight. Keep her curtains closed at all times, understand?"

"All right," Bess said. "If you think it will help her, I will run outside nekked if you say so."

They both burst out laughing.

Stanzy walked through the room and her eyes froze on a small glass bottle on the mantel.

"Bess, is this belladonna?"

"Yes, ma'am. Her mother instructed us to give it to her each night so's she would finally get some sleep."

"Yes, well, in excess, it causes photophobia." She was met with a blank stare. "It makes light painful to her eyes," she explained to Bess.

"Oohh. My poor baby."

Stanzy was relieved to see Lucian wasn't the only person at the manor who cared for this child.

"It is probably the reason Megan cannot tolerate going outside as well. Do not give it to her again."

Bess nodded her understanding.

Constanza sat in front of the little girl, who was now looking up at her from her prone position on the carpet. The girl was dressed in just a shift, no socks or boots of any sort.

"What about her clothes? Surely they have given her clothes, with the opulence of this place?"

Bess strode over to the closet and flung it open to reveal an overwhelming array of dresses, in all shapes and colors. "Oh she has lots of dresses. But she won't keep anything on 'cept that little undergarment. We have to keep washing it over and over. She tears the dresses to shreds if you put them on her."

"Hmm." Stanzy continued to sit in front of Meg and laid on the floor two blocks Lucian had carved and painted in vibrant colors.

She pointed to each block. "Red. Blue." All the while, Meg kept eye contact with her.

"Red." Stanzy repeated as she pointed to the block, and this time brought her hand up and added a sign language motion of her hand while she said it. She followed the same pointing and a slightly different hand motion for the blue block.

"What you doin', Miss Stanzy?"

"It is called sign language. We use it to speak to the deaf. Surely you have met at least one deaf person?"

"No."

"The hand movements take the place of words."

While she explained this to Bess, Meg reached up, grabbed Stanzy's hand and shook it back and forth.

Bess gasped. "She never touches no one. We have to hold her down to bath her and brush that mane of hair. And sometimes her fingernails get so long, they cut into her palm."

Constanza nodded to Bess, then turned back to Megan and repeated the signs and words together. Megan stared at her, but made no attempt to sign. Reaching down, Stanzy placed her hand over the girls when—Whack!

How did she fool me into that?

Pain like she'd seldom felt blazed above her eye and blackness threatened to suck her into it. From a distance she heard Bess yell. "Go get Lucian! Meg done her favorite trick on Miss Stanzy."

A lifting sensation came over her. Next, her hands and feet felt softness all about her—a swaddling feeling. Opening her eyes, she realized she was on Megan's bed. Dear Lucian stood watching her and she gave him a gentle smile. He sank down on the bed beside her, his dark eyes filled with concern. He held out his hand to touch her bruised forehead and winced as if he himself felt the pain.

"What happened?"

"Meg. She hit you with her head, square above your eye. I know this will sound crazy, but I do not think that Meg feels pain. She has bitten herself to bleeding before and never sheds a tear. Your eye looks awful."

Stanzy laughed. "Thank you!"

His face appeared thoughtful for a moment, then smiled. "Constanza, *you* could never look awful to me. You are the most beautiful woman I have ever met."

"Surely you are vexing me, Lucian." She knew she wasn't plain, but she was far from the beauty her sister was and she knew it. She'd learned her role in her family early—she was *the smart* one. Her eyes inadvertently dropped to her left hand, where her index finger was missing.

"There is more to beauty than what the eye sees," he said softly, stroking her cheek. "You are bolder than some men I have known. And my life has been missing something for a long time." He reached over to kiss her on the lips, gently this time.

A shuffling sound from the other side of the room grew louder.

"Oh, my! Well I never thought I would have seen the day! And all these years I thought that heart was made of stone! Well, *c`est la vie.*" Bess stood with both hands on her hips, clucking her tongue.

"What is that ce-la-vee thing you said?" Stanzy asked.

"It mean goes to show you never can tell 'bout folks."

"Bess, that is enough," Lucian said. His voice harsh, but his eyes smiling. Then mildly to Stanzy, "You do have to be vigilant around Meg. She is a very angry little girl."

"I'd be angry too if my mamma and poppa stopped comin' to see me," said the huge woman as she arranged the fresh linen she'd brought into the room.

"BESS! Before you get us both let go."

"Katrina has gone to Bath with the Hopkinses," Stanzy said changing the subject.

"Yes, I know. And I am certain they will pay a call to your friend Edward whilst they are there."

Bess left the room, shutting the door behind her, and Lucian stared at Stanzy, chewing on his bottom lip.

He placed Stanzy's right hand gingerly on the bed and proceeded to pick up her left hand. She was so accustomed to hiding it, she barely even noticed. It wasn't for her own embarrassment, but she'd grown tired over the years of people inquiring about it and her subsequent lies to protect her father.

I cannot breathe.

His thumb gently traced the spot where the finger should have met her hand, and he said, almost shyly, "Are you ever going to tell me what happened here?"

She looked at him. His sincerity almost compelled her to tell the story, but decided it wasn't the place or time.

"Someday."

Stanzy tossed and turned all night with dreams of Edward Teache and Katrina, as screaming muffled cries for help from the deck of the *Freedom* echoed in her head. Faces of the young girls she'd known who had each met a watery grave floated in and out of her consciousness, their heavy dresses pulling them down like jaws to the murky Atlantic bottom.

~ *Chapter Four* ~

"Oh Stanzy, the Hammock House is beautiful! You were daft not to accept Edward's invitation! He has told me of how it once was a place of many grand parties for all sorts of sea captains, and it was built with materials from as far away as Scotland. I do not have use for such tales, but I know you would love to hear all of it! It was built on high ground so that the seamen could use it as a guide from the Beaufort Inlet to wind their way through the deadly shoals, similar to the ones on which we ran aground on our arrival in the banks. He has done nothing but talk of you throughout our stay. He is such a man of the world and has seen so many places. Tortuga and other ports I have never even heard of before.

"Sarah and I have already been to several balls and we may even stay another fortnight.

"I have made the acquaintance of so many ladies here in Bath, as well. Many are married to seafaring men, and pregnancy must be in the water here. I met a Mrs. Drummond, and a Mrs. Thatcher, both of whom are due to deliver at any time. Their husbands are out to sea currently, but I look forward to returning to see if they perhaps have a mate that would meet my standards—my standards, Stanzy, not yours!"

Constanza put the letter down and shook her head. *The silly girl. She'd been silly since the moment she opened her eyes on this world and it didn't help that Father had spoiled her rotten because of her beauty. Her beauty couldn't save us, Daddy. Another of your colossal miscalculations.*

Her father had always hoped Katrina would marry into money and not forget her family after her bags had been packed. In the end though, her beauty hadn't been enough to keep the debt collectors away, nor had it stopped her father drowning his daily sorrows in a tall glass of ale.

Picking up the second letter, her eyebrows knitted with concern. Sealed with a blood red wax, she didn't recognize the handwriting. She opened it with shaking hands, fearing further bad tidings from Bristol, possibly regarding her dear uncle, who was getting on in years.

Her eyes opened and jaw dropped at the contents.

"Dearest Constanza,

"Once you were aboard my vessel, I have had trouble thinking of any other woman. I think you are a good match for me and I am asking for your hand in marriage. I can offer you far more riches than your current station at the plantation and, as there is no father to speak to, I intend to speak to Hopkins about it on my next visit. I will be out to sea for a few weeks, and when I return, I will come to collect my bride!

"Yours,

"Edward Teache"

Chest heaving, her heart pounding so furiously in her chest she felt it might escape her ribcage and drop to the floor, she bellowed into the quiet, "That arrogant idiot!"

What will I do when he comes here? For some reason, that peacock Hopkins seems very intent on keeping Edward Teache happy.

Thank goodness they were all still traveling. She would have some time to sort it all out before their return.

She made her way out of her room and down to the servants' quarters in a daze, not registering any of her surroundings. The life of a governess was a difficult one. She was expected to have the manners of a gentle-woman, but ate and roomed in the servants' quarters. As fate would have it, she wasn't fully accepted by the servants either, as she had access to the master's children.

If not for Lucian, her life would have been very

solitary indeed. He'd been raised on the plantation with all the slaves, so was accepted by them as family. His position as liaison between the two made her welcome in the servants' quarters.

She sat at the table, and Bess placed a cup of tea in front of her. Her hand traced the underside of the table which was smooth, unlike the rough hewn top. It must be an additional table for guests when the plantation became too full for the regular dining room. She wondered if the table had been turned this year at all. The only guests she'd seen the family entertain were Teache and his mates. The only time the Hopkinses did any sort of socializing was when they went into town.

The door opened from the kitchen and Lucian entered, smiling at her. His face was so carefree this morn, he looked ten years younger. Walking to the stove, he scooped oatmeal into two bowls and filled one with milk, and two spoons of sugar.

He set one wooden bowl down in front of her, "I believe this is how you like your oatmeal, Stanzy."

I cannot believe someone actually handed me my breakfast, or noticed my preference for anything. It has been twelve long years since anyone handed me anything other than a baby or a broom.

She felt her eyes well, and tears splatter down onto her cheeks. Since her mother had passed, no one in all these years had ever thought to consider her needs. Lucian's thoughtful gesture touched her so much she ducked her head and wept into her hands. With him she actually felt safe enough to admit she was perpetually frightened, even though her daily attitude conveyed the opposite.

She raised her head and wiped her eyes, watching Lucian's decidedly uncomfortable expression at her reaction to his kindness. He sank into the seat beside her, awkwardly placing an arm around her shoulders.

When she looked sideways at him, she burst out laughing. His expression changed from awkward to utterly dumbfounded.

"Stanzy?" he said very carefully.

"Lucian. I have never seen the likes of you." She leaned and kissed him full on the mouth.

Never losing contact with her lips, he hauled her onto his lap. His hands caressed her hips.

Bess shook her head in astonishment. "My word! Would you two just go on and get it over with! Neither one of you is goin' to be of any use around here 'til you just go on and get together! These folks is puritans, and if they sees you two goin' on like this out where others can see, you two both gonna be outta work!"

When Bess quit speaking, he broke the kiss. His face was serious again, and he gently extricated her entangled body from his.

"She is correct, Stanzy. Puritans can be punished for even caring too much about any one thing, even their own children. They believe God may punish them for attributing too much value to possessions and family. We have to do this right."

He kissed her again, quickly. Then dropped to one knee on the hardwood floor, the noise resonating through the kitchen.

Mouth agape, Bess plopped down the spoon she was stirring the oatmeal with and yelled. "Alfonso! Get in here!"

The elderly man ambled in as quickly as his rheumatism would permit and looked wildly around for trouble. Then seeing Lucian on the floor, he nodded and grinned at Bess.

"Stanzy, I know we have known each other only a month's time, but sometimes in life you just *know*. Would you do me the honor of being my wife?"

He looks so vulnerable. I have never met anyone who could be so self-assured one moment, as when he stood up to Teache, or when he looked so frightened of me, a woman, as if I have the power to strike him down.

She swallowed hard. Never in her wildest imaginations had she thought this day would come for her. Long ago she'd resigned herself to being alone.

"Yes, Lucian, I have never wanted anything more in

my life."

The joy on his face mirrored her own elation. Reaching for her, he pulled her down to the floor. He lost his balance and took her with him, falling in a heap of arms and legs.

Bess guffawed and added, "They are perfectly matched—perfectly insane."

Constanza walked across the dim apartment toward Megan's bed. Bess felt Meg had to be sick as she hadn't so much as ventured out of her bed for a whole day. Her tiny body was wrapped in the blanket so tight, Stanzy was afraid she might smother herself.

Megan began to cry in earnest as soon as Stanzy touched her back. Peering under the covers she saw Meg cradled a doll to her chest. This doll wasn't like the others she'd decapitated or maimed. It was soft, and she desperately clung to it as she sobbed.

I knew she was in there, stuck in her mind...

Empathy was an easy emotion to feel toward this tiny, sick creature whose parents no longer visited her, who perpetually felt uncomfortable in her own skin, and who was unable to communicate even her most basic needs. Life could be crueler than death at times.

Stanzy swiped at her face, surprised at the tears wetting her hand. Groomed from an early age as a physician, she'd been taught to be stoic and logical despite the pressure or situation, and above all else, to assist the patient in feeling safe and cared for. She'd successfully remained emotion-free for amputations, births, and even an occasional death—however, children were different for her.

This child was different.

She'd pierced through Stanzy's protective bubble like a needle through parchment paper.

"Meg. Meg, sit up."

Meg stared at her from under her blanket cave.

Constanza raised her hands and performed the sign 'mama.' Meg sat up suddenly and grabbed Stanzy's hands and shook them. Stanzy quickly performed the sign again, then Meg took her hand and imitated the gesture.

"Yes! Yes! Mama!" Stanzy stood up and shouted an unrefined whoop of glee loud enough to send Bess flying up the stairs.

Then the realization dawned on her. "Honey, I am not your mama."

Meg continued to stare at her and performed the sign again.

"Bess, I am just going to permit her to call me it, as it is the first attempt to communicate I have ever seen."

"She can call you cat vomit if she wants, for all I care. You get her to talk and I will be sure to tell Hopkins it was all your doin'. Then that Teache feller won't have no chance of sweepin' you outta here!"

"How did you know about that?"

"You ought to be more careful where you leave your personal effects layin' open for the world to see. Does Lucian know about the proposal?"

Stanzy cast her eyes down and nipped her lower lip. "No. I haven't spoken of it to him. I didn't want to mar the memory of Lucian proposing to me."

"Only thing that is marred is your dress, from rollin' 'round on the kitchen floor with him. You best tell him soon."

"I will."

Two hours later, Stanzy walked down the stairs, nursing an open wound to her arm where Meg had clawed in frustration when she couldn't comply with her requests. At the kitchen sink, she began to clean the wound, wincing at the burning pain. The door opened and the boys and Lucian emerged from the field.

Arms wrapped around her waist, until he saw what she was doing. "Meg?" he asked pointedly.

"Yes, but Lucian...she is signing...come with me, you have to see her."

The sloop made its way through the narrow azure waterway between Ocracoke Island and the sandbar. To the crew, it had now become known as 'the hole.'

Morning sun rose over the island and the crew—men not accustomed to idleness—was losing patience. One day's wait alone had resulted in three knife wounds and one death.

"Aye, Captain, I can see her approaching!" Beaumont called from his lofty perch in the crow's nest. "She is coming in from the southeast."

The sloop sprang into action, gliding out of the hole and into the Atlantic proper. The small Dutch fleut was no match for the sloop, which began to gain on it immediately.

Beaumont dropped to the deck, making the cabin boy jump with fright. "You see, Johnny, the fleut is a prime target. Cargo is housed in its hull, and it only takes twelve men to man it. There may be twelve guns, but that means each seaman will have to man a gun, with no one left to man the sails," he explained to the young cabin boy.

"Well that is just daft, they are asking for us to come and take their loot."

"Aye! The owners are cheap, and want to pay as little as possible to get their goods to the Carolina's, so that usually means there will be a small crew aboard—" He was stopped short by the sound of gunfire.

"Sir, the flag is red today...the other week we sailed, a black flag was raised...what do they mean?"

"Red means no quarter, boy."

The captain emerged. Although used to his appearance each day, the cabin boy shrank back in fear and awe. The captain had lit his beard on fire—or so it seemed—and his beard grew all the way to his eye sockets, making him look more animal or perhaps devil, than man.

The *Queen Anne's Revenge* began firing on the fleut, and sure enough, it stood still in the water as it returned fire. They approached the vessel within yelling range and the captain bellowed, "If ye surrender yer cargo now, we will let ye swim to shore. If not...well the gate to hell has already been open."

There was a moment's complete stillness in the

water. The only sounds in the silent, close air were the waves licking at the sides of the ship. Then sound ripped through the air as the fleut recommenced firing upon the *Queen Anne's Revenge.*

"Prepare to board and slaughter."

Stanzy pulled the puppies away from their mother one at a time to examine them. "Lucian, these dogs are beautiful. The boys are going to be so thrilled to have them."

"Yes. Ben has been waiting for weeks and asks *every* day if they have arrived. I am sure Will and Lucas will want one, too."

"Well, of course! What self-respecting boy does not want a dog? Lucian, what if we give one to Megan?"

His face clouded and he stared off into the fields of tobacco for a moment as if searching for an answer.

Finally he returned her gaze with a sad expression. "Stanzy, you know I love the little lass like she is my own, but I am afraid she will maim or kill the pup."

"I understand how you feel. But she has never been given a chance, Lucian. She has only been out of that room a handful of times since she was two, and each time accompanied by you. Let me try. I will watch her, and I won't leave her alone with it unless I am certain it is safe."

"All right. But I would keep it close to your chest."

"We have many secrets, Lucian. First, that I am to be your bride, and now a puppy for Megan!"

He leaned over the basket and kissed her hard on the lips. "Stanzy, I know you want to wait 'til everyone is more settled, but I am not sure I can. Let me come and sleep in your bed tonight. I promise to be a gentleman, but I spend half my nights thinking of you anyway. I might get more sleep if I could feel you beside me."

"I will think about it, but we would have to be very careful. You know how steeped in tradition this entire plantation is. Lucian, I need to tell you something."

Here it is. If he is true, he will not doubt me.

His eyes, darting back and forth across the fields,

snapped back to her with such intensity it took her by surprise. "What is it?"

"I received a letter."

"Yes, go on. Speak plainly."

"It was from Edward Teache. He asked for my hand in marriage."

Lucian stood so quickly it knocked her off balance. She was taken aback as he paced to and fro across the school room floor, muttering. "This will not do. No this will not do at all."

"Lucian—"

"How long have you known this?" His eyes went wild and pupils became a pinprick. His dark hair fell across his forehead and he swiped it out of his face in irritation.

"A-about two weeks...I was going to tell you, but I did not want to intrude on our happiness."

"Stanzy, obviously you do not realize the gravity of this situation. Teache is very dangerous; I did not want you to know *how* dangerous as I did not want to alarm you—"

"Alarm *me*? Someone who has been caring for herself and two siblings—one a mere baby—since she was sixteen years old? Who traveled across the Atlantic without male escort? I do not need your protection, I need your honesty!"

"And I yours!" He stormed out of the school, throwing the door open so hard it hit the wooden frame with an earsplitting clatter.

Pulling the smallest pup to her, she nuzzled its fur, taking deep breaths...the boys would be in any minute to start their lessons and she dared not let them see her so vexed.

The sun was a mere amber slit in the sky and an autumn wind howled outside the school room door, warning the world winter was coming. Stanzy had missed the dinner hour, but after the row with Lucian, she had no appetite. Besides, the boys' papers awaited correcting and she needed to analyze her plan of action with Megan. She found contemplation impossible in the estate house, what with the vast array of servants and constant flurry of activity. In the solitary nature of the school cottage, she did her best thinking.

She slid out her mother's old notebook containing handwritten concoctions of herbal remedies and common maladies. Running a hand over it, her fingertips caressed the cover gently.

I miss you so much, Mama.

It seemed so long ago she'd been taken away. Stanzy found it difficult to remember the time before her death. A time when Stanzy would do her best to stay happy despite the drunken rampages and fights that inevitably ensued between her father and mother. She examined her mother's perfect penmanship and traced over it with her fingers.

BANG!

The door burst open and collided with the side of the schoolhouse.

She looked up expecting to see a swirling wind, but filling the doorway, was her supposed betrothed, Edward Teache. Her breath left her chest at the sight of him. Gone was the slicked hair and clean-shaven face. His disheveled hair stuck out at all angles. His beard covered his face up to his eyes and twisted weirdly into strange worm-like tangles. The distinct smell of saltpeter and lime and...gunpowder permeated the schoolroom air.

"Allo, Constanza. I assume you received my letter of intention? Please excuse me looks, I was in a bit of a hurry to get over to StoneWater. Have you collected your bags?"

"Mr. Teache..."

"Edward, now...surely a husband and wife should start by calling each other their God-given names...I have already spoken to Hopkins, and he approves of the match as long as you are still to stay on as his children's teacher." He advanced closer to her.

"I am afraid I am already betrothed to another, Edward."

"How can that be so? I only left you a fortnight ago, and you were well on your way to spinsterhood then...which I cannot understand with one as pretty as you...and your *deformity* does not bother me a whit." That said, his powerful arms swept her into an embrace and he shoved his tongue into her mouth.

Retching, her fists beat uselessly against his bulk. Her hand pushed against his chin, and she vaguely registered hemp ropes woven into that formidable beard.

The sound of the pistol cocking reverberated through the empty schoolhouse.

"Step away from her, Teache. I prefer not to shoot a man in the back, but I will if I have to."

"Ahh...Lucian Blackwell. Well, let me guess... are *you* my rival?" He glared at Constanza. "You chose a farmer over what I could provide for you? And I thought you were the most clever woman I had ever met." He released her, but not before he had wound a handful of her long, dark hair into his fingers. "This is not over."

Lucian kept the pistol cocked and pointed at Teache's head. He followed him out the door, watching him walk away. Pausing at Constanza's side, he said without looking at her, "This all could have been avoided if you'd been forthright with me from the beginning."

Staring out into the starry sky Stanzy couldn't sleep despite the late hour. The rocking chair in Katrina's room had beckoned her, where she sat wondering how her sister fared with the master and mistress of Hawthorne House. She'd been gone for nearly a month and Stanzy missed her terribly, despite their frequent bickering.

Will's loud snoring filtered in from the adjoining bedroom. Tiptoeing to the doorway, she permitted the comforting picture to soothe her anxious soul. Jack lay snoring in unison with his master at the bottom of the bed, and the new pup curled directly under Will's outstretched arm. Well, at least one of us is happy, she pouted. And she hated pouting and people who pouted!

Although she didn't want to admit it, she was still shaken by the encounter with Teache.

The door to the servants' back stairwell flung open, smacking the wall with its force. In charged Lucian with a small frightened man in tow.

"Stanzy, this is Pastor Brooke. He agreed to come and perform our marriage vows."

Well, so much for being quiet. "What, Lucian, have you gone mad? When the Hopkinses return, they are going to be livid."

"No one saw us arrive, but please, we have to make haste!"

"Yes, Lucian has been a friend for years, and when he made me aware of the situation..." The pastor's eyes dropped uncomfortably to her middle.

"Lucian, you told him I was pregnant?"

"I had to! To get him to come tonight, and besides, perhaps by tomorrow morning you will be..."

She stared incredulously at him, but the impulsive fool was smiling from ear to ear, the previous irritation completely forgotten. "I will say it again," she reiterated, shaking her head. "You are like no one I have met before..."

Later, when he laid her onto the bed, she saw his eyes fill with apprehension, or perhaps regret. "You deserve so much better than this, but I am afraid Teache will return. I felt if we were already wed, it would dissuade Hopkins from just turning you over to him, like the coward he is. When everyone knows we are wed, we will have a gathering, with food and music."

Stanzy lay back on the bed and tugged his waist close to her with both feet. "I do not need parties and games. I just need you," she whispered sincerely.

The next morning, she felt him slide over to her again for the third time since last night. He raised onto one elbow. "You are so beautiful."

The door to her room opened. Bess stopped mid-walk and dropped the sheets she carried to the floor.

Worse yet, behind her in the hall, Mr. and Mrs. Hopkins stood, mouths agape, staring at the spectacle of the two of them entwined in the sheets...and one another.

~ *Chapter Five* ~

Lucian sat in front of Hopkins' desk, his fingers fumbling as he tried in vain to lace his shirt. "I already explained this...we are wed!" Raising his hand, he showed Hopkins the ring—for the fourth time. "I know Teache will return and we both know bloody well he does not take no for an answer with anything!"

"Yes, I fear for all on this plantation for what you have done." Hopkins slammed his fist on the desktop. "You should have just let him have her Lucian. This town has any number of women more than willing to bed the likes of—"

The rest of his diatribe was cut short by Lucian's fist colliding with his mouth. A trickle of blood trailed to his chin. He angrily swiped it away.

"That is my wife you are speaking of, you pompous moron! And it is not what *I* did. It was what *you* did. Perhaps if you would have put as much time into the tobacco as the bloody storehouse and cellar full of rum, we would not all be in this quandary in the first place. Yes, I know about all of it. Nothing happens on this plantation that I do not know about. I will finish out the year and crop season here, and then I want what was promised to me—my land. Then I am taking Constanza out of this house. If she decides to continue teaching will be her decision."

He stormed from Hopkins' presence. Kicking open the front door, he left it to blow back and forth in the morning wind.

Pilot flipped his head in the air in protest as Stanzy mounted him in the dim morning light. She adjusted herself in the saddle as he performed a skitterish dance, expressing his dislike at having to leave his barn at four thirty in the morning.

She couldn't sleep. The encounter with Edward Teache the evening before at the schoolhouse had made her realize how terribly vulnerable she was on the plantation. Teache was free to roam unchecked about the land, nay even encouraged to do so by her employer. She felt the rogue could be behind any tree or building on the property.

No doubt, she could depend on Lucian to come to her aid in a heartbeat, but she was also aware that every day, from sunup to sundown, he was miles away in the fields. Far out of earshot of any cries for help.

I am going to conceal a weapon on my person every day. The lecher could show up anytime he has a mind to...with that witless employer of mine.

"Come on, Pilot," she nudged. The horse quickened his gallop.

Momentarily closing her eyes as the wind blew across her face, she savored the feeling of sitting atop the magnificent, powerful creature as he pelted forward. Weaving him along the stone walls that outlined the manor's property, the labyrinth of rocks reminded her of her mother's homeland—Ireland.

She wondered if the architect of these walls had called Ireland his native land as well. From childhood she'd been raised on Irish folklore and tales. Her mother hadn't been a stupid woman. On the other hand, her grandmother had more than likely been insane, not just exceedingly peculiar.

Alone, perched on top of Pilot, seemed to be another way she could think clearly. She was perpetually surrounded by children, or other hired hands. Her mind was in need of solitude. Something vexed her, something keeping her from enjoying the happiness of her new marriage. The dubious problem pricked her conscience like a thorn on a rosebush. She tried to deny the source of the anxiety, but it was time to face it.

Contained in a portion of the letter from Teache that

she'd destroyed after reading it was: *"Ye will be wantin' to accept me offer, for as ye are probably aware, there be curses that happen on women who refuse a pirate's offer to wed. And I be likin' ye too much to hand ye that fate."*

This was a ridiculous notion, she well knew, and her scientific brain, inherited undoubtedly from her father, scoffed every time the concept entered her conscious thoughts. However, her *feelings* kept nagging at her, and a sense of dread drenched her heart as she mulled the pirate's words over and over in her head. *She had to get control of her mind.*

You are being as daft as your grandmother. Stop it you fool! You finally have some happiness, just accept it graciously.

She remembered her mother's extreme behaviors when Stanzy was but a child. Every September, when the Irish festival of Samhain would have taken place in her native land, her mother would make them stay indoors for days at a time, as this was the time the Dollahan would ride. Legend claimed the fairie unstoppable, except for one Achilles heel—gold. Obsession often drove her mother to check outside her children's windows at night, to reassure her tortured mind the piles of coins she placed there remained untouched. Her grandmother had passed down this tradition to her daughter, and although her mother was a Christian, she couldn't shake the customs she'd been raised on. Stanzy's knowledge about fairies rivaled her wisdom on birthing babies. She was delivered the teachings in equal measure, each from her parents' separate views.

Pulling up on Pilot's reins, the horse stopped abruptly. Had she heard something in the dark? The gloaming was coming and a hazy light faintly illuminated the distant ground where the earth met the sky.

It sounded again—the snort of a horse.

Her primitive brain awakened as her heartbeat filled her ears. A horrid recollection arose. Her mother's disjointed portrait of the Dollohan, illustrated at the end of her life, when her mind revolted against sanity. A fairie depicted atop a black steed, his fly-like compound eyes bulging—searching for its next victim. As a child, she completely avoided the room housing the picture.

The snort of the Dollahan's horse is what is heard as he sits outside your gate, bringing with him the announcement of death if his horse ceases its ride.

In the misty distance, Constanza spied him—a cloaked rider, holding a large, round object in his hand at the side of his horse.

It is his head, which he will hold aloft to scan the fields for me, and when he sees me, he will call my name...and I will die, her unchecked brain screamed within her head.

She involuntarily put her fingers in her ears, and still heard the horse's whinny as the rider pivoted to face her. Beneath her, Pilot pranced back and forth and whirled to face the manor from whence he came. His obedience knew its limits, the horse reared and bolted like a shot in the direction of the barn.

This cannot be real. Am I losing my mind? The first time in my life I am happy and now I am going daft? What is next, another fantastic fairie portrait from the next generation of lunatics?

As Pilot whipped her around, from the corner of her eye Constanza caught the rider's hand, rising to lift the round satchel high into the early morning air. Body curled toward his neck, she urged the horse on. Sweat wet her palms, making the reins slip. Pilot's flanks were white with perspiration as the horse fled on instinct.

Who could that have been?

She resolved to tell no one, for fear they would think her mad. Indeed, Father had fastidiously hidden many of her mother's behaviors from anyone outside their household. He knew of her grandmother's mental illness, and the fear that it might be passed on in her mother or his children had been a real concern.

So, she was very reluctant to discuss this incident with anyone. But reconsidering, she felt surely she could ...should...tell Lucian.

Would he really want a mad bride? her brain

purred viciously.

She locked it in the Pandora's box in her mind, which now contained so many secrets she pictured a hairline crack forming in its façade. She decided not to decide. Best to think on it later, when she was capable of more rational thoughts.

Not thoughts of Fairies and Dollahans.

When she heard a horse snorting in the distance, goosebumps covered her entire body.

In the schoolhouse the next day, Constanza held the girl's small body close to her own. She released her and checked the window for what seemed the fifteenth time...where was he?

She gently rocked Megan. Stanzy's face flushed as she thought of Sarah Hopkins. Birthing babies with her father, it had been very clear to her—not all women should be mothers. Maternal instinct was not inherent in every creature, as she'd witnessed too frequently in her lifetime. Many babes had been dropped on their doorstep over the years—babies abandoned by their mothers. Constanza had decided men and women contemplating parenthood should be tested for compassion, as too many were so selfish, their children merely represented a status symbol or another pair of laboring hands. They had no inclination that their role was to love, nurture, and help their children reach their full human potential.

Katrina, for instance, should never have children...

"It is all right, baby," she said soothingly as Meg's eyes darted frantically back and forth. Her hands flew to her ears, and her eyes opened and shut against the bright light. The sunlight still plagued her at times, occasionally making her cry out in pain.

Constanza's gaze was drawn to the chains in the corner of the room. It was her turn to close her eyes.

The door to the schoolhouse opened, and Lucian rushed in, face flushed from running. "I'm here, I am sorry. I was detained by a problem with the water and the fields. Hello, Meg." He moved slowly, dropped to his knee in front of her as he searched her face. "You want to go play?" With his left hand he simultaneously made the sign for play Stanzy had taught him.

They kept Meg between them, each holding a hand, as they walked toward the back field, out of sight of StoneWater.

As they walked, Stanzy reflected on this man who was her husband.

Husband.

Unbelievable.

She'd been sure she was fated to be alone. Facets of his personality continually revealed themselves to her like rings in a tree, each idea larger than the next, but all still part of a master plan.

He is so quiet one might think he never has a clever thought. Quite the opposite. When he finally speaks, I am astounded with his ability to discern the character of others.

"I hope we can get our homestead finished soon," Lucian said. "This is going to be a bad winter."

"Oh, really. Tell me farmer, how is it you are so sure of this?"

"All right, Mrs. Blackwell. You may know a lot about how *my* body works, but as for the seasons and the dirt...well I think there is no contest there."

"Please, amaze me."

"Well, number one, it is almost November and the trees have not shed their leaves as yet. That is a sure sign that this winter will be hard."

Stanzy looked around and indeed the trees were all still sporting the amazing fall kaleidoscope of red, yellow, brown and green. She so loved this season. In England, the seasons changed so quickly that the leaves merely fell off the trees, missing the colorful landscape North Carolina provided.

"Number two, again it is almost November and it is still very *warm*. Number three, the wooly worms are almost completely black, not brown. These are all signs we're in for a bad winter."

"Hmm. I believe you need to come and give the boys

a lecture on the North Carolina climate."

"Well, maybe I will."

Stanzy's head whipped around—a crackle in the underbrush echoed in the still air.

Lucian calmed her. "Don't worry, Stanzy, I have a whole plan arranged. Bess and Alphonse are to alert Ben or one of the boys if the Hopkinses arrive home early from chapel. They know where to find us." Then he changed the subject. "I remember what you said the other night about Megan needing to improve her balance, so..."

An old tree with a massive trunk towered ahead, overlooking the meadow. A newly mounted wooden swing oscillated in the breeze. Meg wrenched free her hands and broke into an all out run for the tree, whooping with nonsensical words—her language as they called it.

Lucian caught up and propelled her tiny body forward, sending her flying into the air. Megan dipped her head backward, smiling from ear to ear. Her long, dark hair fluttered behind her like a bride's veil. Stanzy tore her eyes from Megan to regard Lucian. Tears streamed down his cheeks, or so she thought. She could barely see through her own.

"B-B-B, D-D-D! Megan talk to me!" Stanzy jumped in front of the swing grabbing Meg's legs as they swung to her. For some unexplainable reason, when Meg was moving she could get more speech from her. She thought it something to do with Megan's brain fever.

Megan softly repeated "B-B-B" and tried to sign every motion she'd been taught over the past few months. Pointing to the sky, she nearly fell from the moving swing signing Bird! Dog! Mama! Pa! Sky! Happy! Play!

Lucian wordlessly broke away from the overwhelming situation, and headed toward the rushing river below. Stanzy knew he was trying to compose himself, so she let him go.

"Baby's safe, in her room. She looks up and sees the moon. She will sigh, so will I, as I rock her back to sleep," came the eeriest, wonderful little voice Stanzy had ever heard.

Lucian turned back. She saw her awed expression mirrored on his face for a brief second before she tripped and fell backward to the ground, astonished.

It was the first time Megan had spoken.

~ *Chapter Six* ~

Katrina could hardly sit still. She fidgeted with so much nervous energy her cup shook and tinkled on its saucer as it teetered dangerously close to the edge.

"Katrina, have you seen Mr. Teache? Will he be attending the ball this evening?" requested Emilia, her newly found cohort, whose eyes never stilled. The girl possessed a ruthless talent for picking apart each dress and its wearer as the women flounced across the dance floor.

Her pregnant belly was so large that even sitting was an awesome feat for her.

"No, dear. Edward is still out to sea, but I expect him to return any day...and to be honest Emilia, I believe he may be interested in me! My sister will so not be pleased, but I care not. If it were up to her, I would marry some boring barrister. But I want adventure! I want... passion."

"Oh, well, there is passion with the sailors to be sure." Emilia patted her gargantuan middle. "However, you have to be careful. See Mrs. Drummond over there, well her husband is a seaman as well. And Mrs. Thrumble's husband is a sailor."

She pointed across the room to women nearly as pregnant as herself. Both were sipping tea and holding the characteristically uncomfortable posture of the last trimester.

"You see, our husbands are gone all the time. When they return from sea...well let's just say they make up for lost time. Mrs. Drummond...this is her sixth child in seven years...not counting her two miscarriages."

"Oh my," said Katrina who absentmindedly ran her

hands around her slim waist. Her vanity weighed the scales between a huge mid-section or a married life to an exciting sailor. "I do not particularly want any children. They require so much work. Slaving as a governess has given me my fill of children. Unless I might have my own—then she could deal with the unpleasantness of child rearing. Have you ever met their husbands?"

"No, they are never in port at the same time. We also live quite a distance apart and only come into town for social gatherings."

Katrina barely registered the last three words as a handsome lad in a soldier's uniform bowed in front of her. "May I have this dance, Miss?"

Perplexed, Stanzy sat at her teacher's desk and stared at the papers in front of her, waiting to be corrected. They were not going to correct themselves. Rubbing her temples, she shook her head to clear it; she couldn't focus.

With some difficulty she tried to sort out her feelings about her growing fear of Edward Teache. Could it be that all of the misfortunes occurring since her arrival at StoneWater were somehow connected to *him*? Her rational brain waded through the feasibility of how this was possible...her superstitious side said simply: *The fairies have followed you from your homeland, and wish to torture your newly found happiness. You will be the one to pay for all of your father's horrible mistakes, and deep down you are just like him.*

"No. I am not like him. I choose to do good despite what evil I see around me," she said aloud, slapping the desktop.

Familiar feelings of despair seeped into her conscious mind like an icy draft under a door. Feelings so normal for her, she didn't recognize them at first. Depression cracked open the box of mind memories. Visions of her grandmother flooded her thoughts and her hands flew to her face in a feeble attempt to stave off the images.

Her sixteen-year-old body shivered, but not from cold, as her grandmother led her to Father's study. Gran's bony hand a circlet around Constanza's wrist. She knew it was useless to resist, for the old woman would relentlessly pursue Stanzy until the crone felt her task accomplished. Her reasoning capabilities were lacking before her mental illness had taken hold, but now there was almost no coherent pattern in her thought processes.

They arrived at the study and her grandmother scrutinized her. "Do you see that devil in there? He is the reason my baby is dead. You and your brother and sister need to come back with me to Ireland, away from him, before he kills you, too."

Constanza peered into the dimly lit study at her father's sleeping form sprawled out on his desk of papers. Turning, she gazed into the eyes of a mad-woman. Her head vacillated back and forth looking for a hallucination unseen to everyone except herself.

"I know Father is useless, Gran, but taking Will and Kitty from their home is unacceptable. The only pieces of Mother that remain are locked in this house. In Katrina's nursery, she can still picture Mama sitting in the rocking chair, reading to her aloud, and I..."—she swallowed hard—"I can see her smiling at me from the kitchen in the morning when I woke each day."

"Rubbish, you know the drunk will kill you. He despises both you girls—he loves only the boy."

She had no options. Her father was a drunken lout who provided no love whatsoever. However, he had provided a roof and food for them, and she had respectable employment.

She regarded Gran, and said, "We will not come with you to Ireland."

Her mind trembled with fear as she remembered her grandmother seated in their parlor, staring blindly out the window into the garden. In one of the old woman's worst episodes, she had sat frozen, her arm stuck up into the air reaching for some unseen object. Her face could remain unchanged for days on end. Upon visiting the madhouses with her father, she'd seen the catatonic posturing of many of the patients there— like statues frozen after staring into the face of Medusa—with no way of freeing them from the prisons of their minds.

Shaking her head to clear the memory, Constanza quit the papers. The letter she'd avoided reading sat on the desk. Sarah Hopkins had delivered it to her upon their return, saying Katrina had stayed on in Bath. She picked it up and began to walk toward the cottage.

It amazed her how easily one could settle into a 'normal' life, after so many years of an abnormal upbringing. Each day she spent here was a balm for her soul.

As she approached the cottage, she heard the boys outside getting one last run with their pups before absolute blackness set in. Constanza stepped into her herb garden, which would now have to wait as it had been started too late. She began to run over her mental list compiled from Gerard's plant reference the previous year: mint, lemon balm, lavender, thyme, yarrow.

Next year.

Yes, incredibly, she was to stay here and become a 'Banker.'

Uncle Ellwood was right. You never could be sure where life's road would lead you.

With difficulty she wrenched open the heavy barn door, stopping to let her eyes adjust to the dim light. Picking up the feed, she placed the oat bucket under Pilot's mouth. The back door opened and Lucian entered. His walk was slow and deliberate—like so many things about him. At times his gaze was so intense it made her uncomfortable, but she met it headlong. She knew what was on his mind. It flowed through his eyes like a river of fire.

His arms wrapped about her, and his mouth captured hers. Breathing harder, he led her toward the house.

"Lucian..."

"I thought Bess said it would be better once we were together!"

"No. Now I no longer have to rely on my imagination..."

A middle-aged man watched as the sloop *Adventure* pulled into port in Bath and dock. He'd once overheard someone describe his appearance as unremarkable, which perfectly suited his occupation. His job was to observe—blend in as just another face in the crowd.

The local villagers were all aware of the ship's infamous captain who now stood on deck, formidable and haggard looking. Gone was the oil slicked hair and clean shaven face he'd sported when he caroused the town in search of lady folk. What had replaced it was a mane of wild, black hair and a black beard that had grown in as thick as sheep's wool.

Captain Teache's eyes scanned the milling crowd, and it was obvious he searched for something, or someone. Frustration evident on his exhausted features, he turned to bark orders at the crew, who set to scurrying like the bilge rats they were.

The rumors starting to circulate of the invasion of pirates around the Ocracoke Inlet, where fast, small ships would overtake the lumbering cargo carriers and plunder its crew, were apparently true. Teache's commands resulted in the unloading of countless barrels of the unmarked variety. Many of the crews attacked had been completely obliterated, while others had been marooned on sandbars, depending on their willingness to cooperate with the invasion. The whispering undercurrent of every pub stated the pirate marauder was possibly the devil himself, the bloke often appeared to have his very beard on fire; these were superstitious folk. They assumed the man, if he were not Lucifer, had a deal with the devil, as none of his conquests had failed to date.

The man put away his spyglass and closed the window on the harbor scene. He sat and began in a tidy hand, "Dear Governor Spottswood." He considered how to word the letter. He knew following the pirate would be easy—at least for the next few hours. Teache was a good paying patron of the local brothels and bordellos in and around Bath. If the man slipped his sight, he felt confident he would know where to find him after writing the correspondence.

Stanzy smiled over the pot, stirring the leftover portions from dinner. The boys had gone to bed. As was his custom each night, Lucian was out walking the grounds of StoneWater. He would visit the slave quarters and check on the ill and older ones. He walked a large perimeter of the land around the main house, 'for ease of mind' as he always put it.

She picked up her teacup from the table. Lucian's hasty footfalls echoed on the porch, and the wind forced the door from his hand, banging open. Stanzy leapt, flinging the cup from her grasp. It shattered on the floor in front of her.

His face etched with anxiety, chest heaving, he spit out, "Stanzy, come quickly. It's Meg."

As soon as the words were out of his mouth she caught snippets of crying on the howling wind outside. The screaming could be heard across the whole of StoneWater. Wails whipped in and out of earshot as the North Carolina wind threatened another fall storm.

Running flat out across the courtyard, the rain began to fall hard and fast. By the time they reached the servants' entrance in the kitchen, the childish howling was perfectly clear, and they were completely deluged.

Constanza slipped on the water she'd dripped onto the back servants' staircase and fell hard onto one knee. Several steps ahead of her, Lucian turned and ran back to help her.

Frantically she waved him on. "Go. Go to her!" The intensity of pain let her know she'd sprained if not broken her ankle. Hobbling up the stairs in desperation, she gritted her teeth against the throb.

The pup she'd recently entrusted to Meg lay dead on

the top step. She stepped over its pathetic corpse and headed toward the sound of the screams. Astounded at the sight before her, she stopped dead in her tracks.

Meg thrashed about just as she had that first day Constanza had laid eyes on her. The girl's screams were accented by throaty growling. Tied to an examining table, leeches littered her tiny body. A man leaned over to peer into her eyes. Meg violently bit his arm with all of her might and blood immediately leaked from his torn flesh onto the table.

Lucian's hands flexed and opened in a frenzied sort of way, while Bess restrained him—her massive form quaking with sobs as she stared at Megan.

"What is going on here?" Stanzy said with a calm she didn't feel.

"I am the patient's attending physician. And who are you?"

"I am her governess and caretaker."

"Well, we have everything under control here." He mopped his forearm which was now bleeding so badly, the soaked cloth dripped crimson.

"You are going to need that sewn. My father was a physician and I was trained as one as well. My mother was a healer. I can stitch it for you. Why is Meg restrained? What have you given her?"

"I have reinstituted the belladonna and added wormwood in small doses, of course, to attempt to calm her animal-like behavior. I need her immobile to administer the bleeding for impurities."

"Begging your pardon, sir, we have had her off the belladonna for several months and she has not been bled since your last visit. She has been doing very well."

"Impossible. Look at her. She is a beast, a creature at best."

Heat flushed Stanzy's neck and face as she bellowed, "She is a child. A girl, in case you have not noticed. A *sick-little-girl!*"

Lucian made another lunge in the physician's direction, and still restrained by Bess, he yelled over Meg's wails, "She has begun to speak! You have no idea what you are talking about! She looked practically normal 'til you started all this again!"

"Are you, farmer, attempting to tell me how to treat my patient? This wretch is not capable of speech, nor does she understand it. I have recommended she be taken to the asylum in Bath."

"Over my dead body will she go to one of those places! I know her, maybe better than anyone. I have taken care of her since she was a year old, and I have never seen her so well, and now to see her lose her senses again...take off those bloody leeches!" At last wrenching away from Bess, he ran to the table and started ripping the creatures off her tiny legs—one by one.

Stanzy limped to his side and removed the disgusting blood-filled creatures from her arm. "We truly have made some wonderful progress with her. We—"

Abruptly snapping his bag shut and gathering his implements, he said scathingly over his shoulder, "Yes I can see that. I will inform Mr. Hopkins that my services are no longer required here. I can see you have everything under control."

After bathing the areas the leeches had been attached, Megan finally quit screaming. Stanzy cradled her on her lap in the rocking chair by the fire.

"Meg. Megan. Look at me."

The little girl's eyes were blank, unseeing. She'd retreated to the place in her mind that was far more safe and happy than the world she lived in.

Lucian sat at the window, his head in his hands.

"Megan, come back to us...oh, Megan." Constanza's voice cracked and she began to cry.

But she continued to rock and sing to her. "Baby sleeps in her room, she looks out and sees the moon..."

The baby was cradled in her arms when she heard her father's footsteps as he entered the house. Bleary-eyed she looked outside and realized it must be close to three in the morning. Quietly as possible, she stood anchored to one spot, not daring to move a muscle. Often when Father returned from the pub his mood was argumentative, and on one occasion he had knocked her unconscious. All in the name of Mother's untimely death. From time to time, Stanzy heard weeping from his room, usually on nights such as this, after a long evening of indulgence.

She silently prayed Will wouldn't awaken and begin to cry, for she knew it would start a situation she couldn't stop. She held her breath until she heard his door click and lock.

Dazed by the dream, Stanzy started where she slept by the fire. She looked around until place and time returned to her foggy mind.

Meg had moved from her arms to the hearth rug by the dying fire. Picking her up, she placed her shivering form in her bed. She searched the room for Lucian, but he was gone. She couldn't think of leaving Meg tonight. Quietly she moved the rocker by Meg's bed and gently, but tightly, held her little hand until she dozed off again.

The sun rose as Stanzy opened the door to the cottage, and plopped herself down at the kitchen table.

"Stanzy, I have to go and lie down for just a few hours, or I will be of no use to anyone. Hopkins is due home today from the ports. I will go to see him as soon as he arrives," Lucian said groggily, automatically stoking the fire over and over.

"Go ahead. I may join you shortly."

He nodded his acquiescence.

Constanza stared at the letter she'd been loath to open for what seemed like days on end. A certain dread had come over her when she'd received it.

Finally, she broke the seal. The aroma of Katrina's fragrance permeated the kitchen from the perfume-soaked parchment. Her sister's perfect handwriting, so opposite from Stanzy's own chicken scratch, came into full view as she removed the letter from its envelope.

"Dear Stanzy,

"All is well with my governess position at the Hawthorne's. The children are insufferable, but most children are to me as you know.

"I do not think I will have to be a governess for long, however. I have many suitors in Bath and am sure within the next few months will have made a smart match; then I will no longer have to be a governess.

"One of my suitors is Dear Edward. He has returned from sea, and we have dined at Hammock House many times over the past fortnight. To be honest, Stanzy, I know that Lucian is handsome, but to pass up such an exciting fellow as Edward must have been difficult. Not to mention he has so many more investments than Lucian."

"Oh yes. Very difficult," Stanzy said sarcastically, at Katrina's colossal inability to discern character. She continued reading.

"I do hope that he does not want children though. I have decided that would definitely not be the right course for me.

"Come to Bath soon and stop laboring so hard. And bring Will, I miss him.

"Warmest Regards,

"Katrina"

Stanzy put her forehead on the table and managed to shake it back and forth only twice before she fell dead asleep.

Stanzy heard it before she felt it. The bone saw had ripped through the tibia and fibula and had just finished its way through the gastrocnemial muscle when she shuddered. Just a tiny burning sensation… then nothing.

She retracted her hand, from under the amputee patient's knee, and held it up in shock and horror. Her index digit hung dangling by a lone sliver of flesh, and blood edged down her arm—not pouring, just taking its time.

She staggered backward and tried to get her

father's attention, but it seemed she'd been momentarily struck dumb.

"Stanzy, what are you doing? I have to finish with the soleus...you know that..." While still speaking he looked up at her. All of the color emptied from his hazy face.

"Oh, poppet. The saw must have slipped, you did not even cry out. Come here quickly."

Even as he said it, the patient on the table began to rouse.

"Bloody...Maura!" he bellowed. Her mother came in quickly through the office doors. "Help Constanza, stitch her up. I have to deal with him or we may lose him."

She awoke and flexed her left hand, which was still sans index. She shook her head and let it sit in her hands while she waited for the fear from the dream to ebb away. Finally relenting, she dragged herself into the bedroom and joined Lucian—already snoring quietly—and gave in to desperately needed sleep.

The afternoon sun's rays were fading. Wincing with every step, she willed her feet to ascend the steps to Meg's apartment. In her exhaustion, she'd only just risen, mortified to have slept the day away. Reaching the landing, she eyed the huge barrels housing Meg's water and milk so the house staff wouldn't have to make innumerable trips to the estate kitchen. Meg was rarely left unattended, even for short periods, as she could be massively destructive. Stanzy maneuvered around them, and stubbed her toe. Half laughing, half crying, she swallowed the expletives poised to fall off her lips. Abruptly, she remembered last night—Meg's pup lying dead on the step. Now nowhere in sight, she assumed a house servant had removed it. Had Megan killed it?

Inside the child's room, Meg rocked back and forth by the fireplace, holding her tattered soft doll, mumbling unintelligible words to herself. She didn't look up to see who had entered.

Bess' huge frame was bent over sweeping what looked like shards of broken stoneware into a pile.

Stanzy felt her eyes go wide. The apartment had been ransacked. Dolls lay strewn everywhere—one still smoldering in the fire—many with the faces chewed off. Meg's bedding, all over the floor in a heap, had been shredded into long yards of material. The draperies, which kept the room dimly lit, had been pulled from the windows. As a result Meg sat with her eyes closed.

"Oh, Bess, why didn't you send for me?"

"It ain't the first time she done this, Miss Stanzy. She just been a bit more behaved since you started caring for her."

Stanzy glanced up, registered the cut on Bess' face. "That will need cleaning."

"It is fine. See what you can do for my baby. She been rocking like that for going on two hours now. And she can't say a word today."

Megan's door swung open and Mrs. Hopkins swooped into the room, her maidservant scurrying behind. Her beady eyes swept around, assessing the situation before her.

Those eyes remind me of a hawk searching for its prey.

"Oh, my word! I go away for a month and the likes of you think you can slack off your duties to this household. I will not stand for it! Look at the state of this place!"

Her blue orbs fell to Megan. "She looks exactly as she did the last time I saw her. What are you doing during these *lessons* we are paying you to perform?"

Constanza tasted the familiar pungency of metal in her mouth that she always experienced during feelings of rage. "When was the last time you saw her, Mrs. Hopkins? I will have you know your daughter was speaking and using sign language to convey her wishes! She is progressing in her ability to communicate. This fiasco you see in front of you is a result of *your* physician's treatment and trauma. Prior to his visit, she was doing wonderfully."

"My husband consulted some important men of our church in Bath, who believe she may be possessed."

"*Possessed*? She is ill! She is a very sick little girl, who is capable of getting better if you just permit me more time with her."

"Her physician has made the recommendation that we put her in the asylum near Bath, which we are considering. You have a few more months to show me some progress, or she will have to go." The woman's eyes were blue fire, showing no compassion whatsoever as she scornfully stared at her daughter rocking on the hearth floor.

Turning on her heel, the mistress of StoneWater exited the room, slamming the heavy door behind her.

"Evil, wicked, loathsome, stupid creature!" Stanzy spat and stomped her foot on the floor, grimacing as pain jolted her injured ankle.

Bess put the broom aside and stared at the floor in front of her, shaking her head quietly.

Stanzy plopped down onto the rocker. "She just wants Megan out of here because she is a burden and does not fit in with her *perfect* southern hospitality home. Oh! Women should have to have a license to bear children, with compassion being a prerequisite. There ought to be a test for maternal instincts! I will not let her go. I will not!" Despite herself, the tears came and Stanzy wailed out loud, hands hiding her face.

After a few moments, tiny hands pulled at Stanzy's and uncovered her face. Meg crawled onto her lap. A feeling, one fiercer than any she'd ever known, burned in Stanzy's chest.

She quietly whispered, "They will have to kill me first."

~ *Chapter Seven* ~

Abernathy Hornigold leaned against a wall in the alley, and checked his watch for the fifth time this hour. Finally the door to the bordello opened, and two drunken men weaved their way into the street, but *not* the man he was seeking. How long could the wretch be in there? It had to have been three hours already.

He debated moving his position when the huge fellow lumbered down the stairs. Two women waved to him from a second-story window and the marauder wobbled across the street to his horse tethered to a railing.

Hornigold followed Teache to Hammock House, once again positioning himself a distance away so as not to be noticed. The appearance of the man who walked out the door was astounding. Having gone inside only an hour before, Teache's hair was now slicked back, beard all but gone, and the man was smartly dressed. Hornigold almost wanted to get closer to verify this was the same man.

Teache disappeared into his carriage. The driver proceeded down the street and made a turn to the left, where Hornigold had followed him previously. He guessed Teache was headed for the Hawthorne's estate, where he would call on the governess.

Sure enough he entered the mansion and Abe waited, biding his time. Teache strode out with a breathtaking, full-bodied creature adorning his arm. The pair walked down the front entrance stairs and turned into the garden. Having seen enough, Hornigold scribbled in his notebook, clucked to his mount and set out on the road back to Bath.

At three in the morning, Stanzy sat in her chair by the cottage fireplace, rocking and cradling the blanket she'd intended to take as a present to Megan before the fiasco when everything had all gone to pieces.

Uncontrollable tears endlessly spouted from her eyes as she rocked. After so many years of being stoic at her dysfunctional home in England, she actually felt safe and free to express emotions she'd repressed for years.

For so many years I had to be the shoulders on which all troubles rested—the rock for Mother, and Will and Katrina. I was the one who had to make it all right, or at least as normal as possible, after Father had been on a binge. Or be the one forced to save his reputation as he treated patients intoxicated, correcting his medication errors. Those days had felt as if they would never end.

When one's reality was so grim and it appeared there was no foreseeable way out, the mind found ways to survive—it formed little pockets or walls where bad memories could be locked away, so the conscious mind could function.

Now that she was safe, many walls were crumbling. Frequently, Constanza found herself weeping alone. It upset Lucian terribly to see her distraught, so she tried to hide it from him. One night he discovered her weeping, and, unable to help, had almost shed tears himself. So, rather than place him in that position, she suffered alone.

Megan.

What was she going to do about her? She'd broken a cardinal rule of physician and teacher alike—do not get emotionally involved—but she loved this little girl, and there was no turning back. For the first time, she could actually consider having children of her own. She'd sworn she'd been a mother since fourteen, and thought that would do, thanks.

I definitely want a child with Lucian.

Quickly, she headed into their bedroom, wiping the

tears from her face, and crawled under the covers beside him. He didn't stir. She crawled on top of him and kissed him on the mouth until he woke.

"What's this?" he asked, slightly confused and not fully awake.

"You are dreaming, go back to sleep," she said as she yanked at his night shirt.

"Well, then, I hope I do not wake up."

The knock at the door was loud.

Stanzy felt Lucian crawl over her half sleeping form. She stretched her body as she struggled to awaken. "Who is it, Lucian?" She looked outside at the darkness and shook her head.

"I cannot imagine. It must be calm of day," was his quiet response.

It took a minute as she used her Outer Banks to English translation dictionary in her head. "Ah...it must be five in the morn."

She searched for something to slide over her night dress and padded across the cold floor at her husband's heels.

Lucian opened the door. Ian Hopkins stood outside on the stoop. Gone was his jaunty, standing-still bounce. His countenance was grave.

"May I come in?" he asked almost inaudibly.

Stanzy watched her husband's shoulders loosen as he let down his guard. Justifiably so—Hopkins looked a man sentenced to the gallows.

"Come in, Ian. Please sit down."

Stanzy put coffee on to brew. In most families, the wife would leave the room and allow the men to discuss important matters. However, to quote Sarah Hopkins: "This is the most unorthodox marriage I have ever seen!" She sat next to Lucian at the table and he absently reached for her hand.

He always takes my hand with the deformity. He does not want people to stare at it. Somehow I know it is not because he is embarrassed, merely that he wants to protect me from questions about it. All this I know just by the way he looks at me.

Lucian *expected* her to be involved in all important decisions. "What is going on?" he prompted Ian.

"Pardon my early intrusion, but several important matters have come up that need to be handled with haste. My wife and I have decided Megan is to be moved, in the next fortnight, to an asylum near Bath." Then addressing Stanzy, he said, "I wanted to be sure our arrangement with you as governess for the boys is still intact. I know Lucian and you plan to move to your own homestead after the end of this season."

His eyes didn't resemble his wife's vacant stare. Quite the contrary, the level of sadness in them was almost difficult to gaze upon. He cast them to the tabletop while uttering this rehearsed speech. Stanzy couldn't help but think that this wasn't his idea.

You weak fool! Do not listen to that shrew of a wife!

"Please sir, do not send her away. Prior to the physician's visit, she was doing so well! We even heard her speak!"

Ian Hopkins' head shot up so fast it startled her. "Impossible. It is cruelty to even suggest such a thing to me! I have not heard her speak since she was one year out—"

Lucian interrupted. "It is true, Ian. I heard her as well. Stanzy is making great strides with her. But she and I need more time."

Ian's eyes darted back and forth between the two of them like a frightened animal. "Really, she spoke...what did she say?"

"She sang a song, a lullaby."

Eyes watery pools, he stood, walked to the door and stared out the window. His unblemished hands absently rubbed the back of his neck.

He turned back. "All right. I will do what I can with Sarah. She is intent that the asylum is best for Megan, but I will tell her this news."

Under the table, Lucian gently squeezed Stanzy's fingers in an attempt to restrain her mouth. He knew her so well and could imagine what would blurt out after hearing this proclamation.

"There is something else—one of the slaves is very ill and in need of medical attention. I have sent for the doctor, but I believe he is currently out of town. I was hoping you would go and look in on the slave quarters and make an assessment of the situation."

"Yes, of course, straightaway." Bidding Mr. Hopkins good-bye, she hurried to the bedroom and began to dress. From behind the closed door she heard Lucian.

"I will be taking Stanzy to Nags Head within a fortnight to meet my aunt. As we married in haste, she was not able to meet my family. Can you manage for a bit without me?"

"Of course, Lucian. Take your time. Everything will be here waiting when you return. Go and enjoy your wife. She is a remarkable young woman."

The ship was sinking.

The hole from the cannonball filled with water as the battle on the upper deck raged on.

The crew of the *Adventure* had overtaken the *Memorial* and unwittingly destroyed part of their booty via the blast. Kegs of rum rolled into the waves as the deck tipped closer and closer to the surface of the water.

The captain of the *Adventure* charged the first mate of the *Memorial* and plunged his sword into the man's torso with deadly skill and accuracy. He turned, searching for *his* first mate. He pulled double pistols from his bandoliers and finished off the only remaining member of the *Memorial* crew in a few seconds time.

"Salvage the cargo!" he bellowed. The crew scurried like bilge rats at the sound of his voice.

He had given the *Memorial's* crew the option of surrender. In that case, he would have plundered the cargo and marooned them. But the proud fools had chosen to fight.

In the storm Abernathy sat waiting by the harbor, watching the *Adventure*, which had docked hours earlier. He wrung his hands at the thought of concluding this deplorable assignment. He'd been following said captain for greater than six months to date, bearing witness to many suspicious circumstances, such as his ships leaving port and returning with all manner of cargo. This would be followed shortly by stories from the locals. Reports about ships that were expected to dock soon, having been raided by pirates only days before their arrival at the Banks.

Almost at the end of this assignment, it couldn't come fast enough. His heart longed to return to Virginia, and his life and post there, which undoubtedly led to why he was going to take this risk tonight.

The sound of the crew dispersing echoed in the night. The last of the seamen finally departed the vessel down the plank to the harbor proper. Five minutes later, Hornigold quickly ascended the plank onto the ship. Being an expert sailor, he lowered himself swiftly into the hull and wandered through the dark as he lit a candle.

Rum.

His grandmother's voice echoed in his head: 'Devil's drink.'

Barrels and barrels of rum lined the ship's cargo hold. There was a dank, rotting smell underneath it all he found disquieting. He began to search through the rows of barrels, not quite sure what he was looking for.

As he took his next step an accompanying squish and the feel of something soft underfoot caused him to leap into the air and knock his head on a beam. He whisked the candle down so fast he feared it would extinguish. A pool of rum leaked onto the floor. Afloat in it were at least twelve dead rats. The stench was so great he juggled the candle and almost caught himself on fire. Gingerly stepping over the rotten mess, he was alerted to sounds on deck.

Voices overhead. Drunken men. Men descending into the hold.

"Blast," he whispered to himself, extinguishing the light.

"Well, sir, I was wonderin' when Mr. Drummond,

Mr. Thrumble, and Mr. Thatch are going to be in port? I have seen all their wives and their middles are all about to whelp at the same time as far as I can tell!" said a surly, slurring voice.

"I care not for any of those men, as my only concern is for the desire of my eyes...Miss Katrina Smythe of Hawthorne House. I believe she will be mine in matrimony by the end of the month, if not in flesh before then!"

"Oh ye are a sly dog with the womenfolk—you are always gone a gal-in."

Abernathy moved back, crouched behind a stack of barrels, and held his breath as they passed his row.

Constanza turned *again* attempting to focus the boys' attention on the math lesson. It was painfully slow going this afternoon.

She assessed her students. Ben stared out the window into the field, probably watching for his father. Will worked on the problem, but she could see beside him on the desk a drawing of the new horse they had recently acquired, now in the barn. Then there was Lucas. The boy's attitude was that he should receive the best grades, as his father paid her salary. But she showed no prejudice and graded him on par with the other boys. They were all about the same grade of student, and they were all *boys* through and through.

They wanted to ride horses and swing from the rope in the barn into the hay, *much* more than learn French or writing. She understood this and tried to keep the lessons interesting for them, but today even her best efforts failed.

"All right, boys, I think we will end a little early today."

Before she'd finished the sentence they were out the door, probably afraid she would reconsider. Smiling to herself, she shook her head.

A post rider handed Lucian a package as he stood on the front pizzer of their cottage. She lifted up her skirts, showing her boots. Running toward him, he laughed out loud at her and shook his head. She was happy he found her unconventional behavior comical, and she believed him when he told her it was one of the reasons he loved her.

"What is it?" she said breathlessly.

"I don't know. It is addressed to you, Miss Smythe."

"That is Mrs. Blackwell to you, sir."

She took the package and shook it. "Maybe my Uncle Ellwood forwarded me one of my books. Oh! I do hope as I miss them all so much."

She tore it open and froze.

Lucian, rocking in one of the many chairs littering the porch, stopped. "What?"

She didn't reply. She extracted a necklace from the box and held it up for him to see. A diamond gemstone dangled at the end of it. As she held it, it swayed back and forth in the breeze.

Inside, they sat facing one another at the table. Each one as cross as the other with the content of the letter, which now lay between them like a line drawn in the sand.

"Miss Smythe,

"I know you have told me you have married that farmer, but I refuse to accept this. Here is a token of my deep and abiding wish for you to consent to be my wife. I told ye before that I could attend to your financial needs in no uncertain terms. It is no feat to have more money than a sharecropper, one step above an indentured servant.

"I beg you to reconsider. If you do not, please keep the necklace to remind you of me. When I see you wear it, I will know you are thinking of me when you look at him.

"Yours,

"Edward Teache"

After reading it again, Lucian dropped it on the table. "Stanzy, darling, you cannot be serious."

"Do you know how much I could buy for Megan with this? I will sell it and use the money to help her."

"No. I do not feel right about it. Everything about him, including this trinket is...*vile*. No good will come from it."

She stared at him for a while. Stanzy didn't believe it was jealousy on which he based this decision, but that he truly believed Teache wicked.

"All right, I will find the address of his beloved Hammock House and send it back to him."

Katrina sat waiting on the window seat, staring out into the darkness. Edward was late, which she was accepting as the norm for him. The man more than made up for it with his gifts and exciting places he whisked her off to, removing her far away from the demands of being a governess.

If she married him, she just *knew* a life of adventure awaited her...after all, he was forever traveling and surely he would take her occasionally on his merchant trips, so she could see the world he spoke to her about. Her image reflected back to her from the window and she admired her long curls. Her long-lashed eyes fell to the locket Edward had given her. It shone and glimmered whenever she was in the sunlight.

Katrina contemplated the idea of giving herself to him, even though they were not yet wed. She smiled slightly, thinking of her sister's mortification, but she wanted to assure Edward's love, and so what if she did become pregnant? Well, then he would certainly have to stay with her, wouldn't he? And she was sure he could afford a governess for the child, and then she would be free—free from the job she despised, and into a life of excitement!

Yes. With his next advance, she wouldn't protest as she had previously. The act would be her insurance policy. And deep down, the fact that Edward chose her over Stanzy, made the match all the more sweet.

The clippety-clop of horses' hooves as the carriage passed through Hawthorne House gates awoke her from her reverie as Dear Edward approached. It was true, he wasn't as young or as handsome as some of her other suitors, but in him she imagined security.

The priest made his way into the apartment with a flourish, followed by two altar boys dragging incense tins on chains, swinging menacingly about behind them. Muttering incantations in Latin, he walked toward Megan who trembled uncontrollably at the sight of him. The tiny girl clung to Bess with all of her might.

"Please, the smell of that will drive her wild, and the bell...please do not hit that bell...she cannot stand loud noises."

At her teacher's desk, Stanzy examined the boys' most recent writings and smiled. Their studies progressed well, and her chest filled with pride for each one of their accomplishments. Looking out the window, the sun was low in the sky. A lump formed in her throat as she realized Lucian hadn't returned for her. He was never late.

After a lifetime of hardship, her mind was suspicious of happiness. As if to say 'you do not deserve it,' or 'it will not last.'

You know you will never be truly happy. You are cursed. You do not need Edward Teache for that. Everything and everyone you touch will be doomed.

She forced the thoughts back into her mind-box, and swallowed the bile rising to the back of her throat. "You are being ridiculous," she chastised herself aloud.

Walking to the window to view the main house, she saw shadows dancing violently in the window. It was Megan's room.

"Oh, no. What now? Can't they just leave the child alone?" she said to the wind as she sprinted toward the mansion.

Opening the servant's door to Megan's apartment, she was just in time to see Lucian's fist connect with Hopkins' chin. His thin body fell to the floor with a whump, and didn't stir.

The priest's expression was grim as he stooped and quickly started gathering his belongings.

"I told you she is sick!" Lucian bellowed, an uncharacteristic savageness in his eyes and voice. His hands shook as if with palsy, as he strode over to Hopkins who was rousing on the floor. Hands pumping, he stood glaring down at Ian's stirring frame.

"I will have you thrown in jail! You impetuous glorified farm hand!" shrieked Mrs. Hopkins, launching her tiny frame at Lucian. "I do not know why my ridiculous father favored you so!"

Ian Hopkins gained his footing, balled his fist and blindsided Lucian who was holding Mrs. Hopkins at arm's length. Lucian toppled backward, feet kicking out and upending a pot by the fire.

Fists, blood and spit and every cuss ever uttered filled the air of the child's apartment.

"Stop it! Both of you! You are upsetting her even more!" yelled Stanzy from the floor, where she crawled her way around the fight to cradle the bawling girl in her arms.

"Stop!" an unfamiliar voice called.

Everyone in the room froze as all heads turned toward the fireplace hearth.

"Stop, please," said Megan in a voice no louder than a murmur this time. A tear cut its track down her dirty cheek.

Stanzy burst into tears, and saw Bess was hiccupping sobs. Even Sarah's eyes shone with unshed tears. Ian Hopkins fell to his knees and cradled his head, but Lucian...Lucian just smiled. Even as the blood trickled from the side of his mouth, he made no move to wipe it. His face gleamed with the expression of a proud father.

"There's my girl. Don't you go away again," he whispered.

~ *Chapter Eight* ~

The baby wouldn't stop crying. Stanzy lifted Will from his pram and held his tiny body close to her chest when she realized the child burned with fever.

"Oh no, oh no," she said, performing a balancing act of holding him on her shoulder and stoking the fire at the same time.

He wailed in protest at the adjustment in her arms.

"Shh! Shh!" she consoled as teardrops dribbled to her cheeks. Cradling Will again, she pelted down the hall to her father's room, the familiar smell of stale spirits made her quiver with anger.

"Father! Father, please wake up. It's Will, he is sick. He is burning up." She tried to rouse him with one hand. He didn't stir.

Her chest heaved and hiccupped out of control. Laying the baby at the foot of the bed, she shook her father with both hands. "Daddy! You good for nothing drunkard! The son you have always wanted is sick and he is going to die just like Mama if you do not help me!"

Katrina entered the room and attached herself to Stanzy's leg, her bawling adding to the orchestra of pain.

"Daddy, please," Stanzy said without much hope now.

Leaving the room, dragging her sister on her leg behind her, she tried to keep Will as covered as possible. All three cried in unison as they descended the steps to the kitchen.

Constanza shakily sat up in bed, drenched in sweat. Lucian quickly wrapped his arms around her. He whispered sleepily, "It was another nightmare. You are safe with me now."

"No, I am not safe! I cannot rest any longer 'til I see Katrina. I know she is in trouble. I have been fooling myself. That girl was born for trouble."

"All right, we will go to Beaufort on our way to Nags Head if you like, but we cannot go anywhere now, it is three in the morning and we can't leave the boys."

Wordlessly, she got up and padded through the kitchen into the boys' bedroom, where the gentle sound of snoring filled the air. Will was getting too old for her to sleep with, but she didn't care. She *had* to feel they were safe in order to sleep at all. Crawling into his bed, she held him tight, as she'd done since his violent entrance to this world. Benjamin would be ribbing him for days over her coming into their room, but she didn't give a whit.

"Megan, look at me, not outside!" Stanzy turned the girl's face with her hand, attempting to hold her attention.

"Watch. M, O, T..." Stanzy's fingers made the letters as she spoke. "You do."

The little girl sat stubbornly, arms folded across her chest.

Megan signed, "Play."

"No...no play, until we do five letters."

Megan responded by squeezing her eyes tightly shut, shaking her head back and forth so rapidly Stanzy felt dizzy.

Ropes were no longer required to restrain Megan. She sat during her lessons of her own volition. She did, however, rebel daily with the length of her lessons. The little trickster was as obstinate as her teacher.

They had sat at odds, at times for two hours, while Stanzy insisted Megan finish *two* letters.

Megan smiled at her for a moment, and then pointed to her ears and put her hand over her mouth—the sign for deaf and mute.

"Oh, no, you are *not* deaf, and hardly mute as I

endured your wailings when I first arrived at StoneWater—you tricky little sprite. We have to finish Megan. Please try."

Megan finally placed her fingers into the shape of an M, followed by the other two letters Stanzy had requested.

Some days it seemed Megan had no control of her own body, and though she might wish to comply with a task asked of her, the girl simply couldn't get her limbs to obey. This often led to full-blown temper tantrums, at other times to crying jags. Stanzy would hold her, and take Megan's hands in her own to assist the child in making her own body move.

Picking up a quill, she extended it out for Megan to take from her outstretched hand. Her face screwed up in a scrunch, her chest started heaving. Stanzy prepared for the howl. Megan detested writing of any kind as well as drawing.

Constanza continued to offer the quill. Finally, Megan reached out, grabbed it, snapping it in half, again shaking her head wildly back and forth. Stanzy put her head on the tiny table and rocked it back and forth in imitation of Megan. Laughing out loud, Megan began to rock her head in time with Stanzy's.

Conceding defeat for the moment, Stanzy grabbed the girl under her armpits, and swung her around in circles in the center of the room. Megan squealed with delight. Stanzy had discovered that if she gave Megan some physical movement prior to trying a school task, her performance and attention increased threefold.

"Now sit!"

The girl laughed and signed, "Eat."

"No! Stop it! You are as bad as the boys!"

She held up drawings Lucas and Ben had sketched one evening for her to use while teaching Megan. Both boys were beautiful artists, whereas Stanzy couldn't even draw a circle properly.

Holding up the picture, she said, "What is it?"

Meg hid her face in her hands, one eye peeking out between her fingers.

Stanzy waited quietly, refusing to move an inch.

"Tree."

"Yes! It is a tree!"

She held up another card.

"Dog."

"Yea!" Stanzy said, smiling in approval.

Bess came into the room from the stairwell. Megan shot up from the table, sprinted to the center and twirled in circles around the room. Then she proceeded to run circles around Bess.

"Bess!" Megan shouted.

"Ahh! You little—"

"Now, Bess," said Stanzy. "You do not want Meg to hear any words that you would not want her to repeat!"

"Don't you think it odd, I am being summoned for this birth?"

Lucian sat beside her, stoic and silent as usual, but somehow his warmth always shone through the quiet. He could convey more meaning in one silent look than many of the charmers she'd met in her day, with all of their flowery sonnets and lofty promises.

"Yes, but I am sure they are reputable if Ian requests it."

Acquaintances of Hopkins were set to deliver their first child. Their regular surgeon was out of town, and he requested Stanzy attend the birth. Despite the late hour, Constanza offered her assistance. Lucian was now complaining about this unnecessary detour on their journey to Nags Head, but she assured him the birth would only detain them, at most, one day.

The wagon rumbled to a stop in front of the designated address. Lucian turned to her. "If you do not mind, I will wait for you here. Should you need anything, just send for me and I will come in straightaway. I have only been witness to one birth, and have to admit it is not an easy thing for me to watch..."

"You know full well most gentlemen are not welcome in the birthing room. Not even the husband! So I am proud of you that you saw Benjamin's birth."

Lucian swallowed hard. "Yes, well, as I said, I felt completely helpless. There is no worse situation for me, where I must bear witness to an act of pain, and I am rendered useless."

The air was so still it felt thick.
It is so quiet. Too quiet.
Either the child or the mother has died. It feels like a tomb.

A crooked man stepped into the vestibule. His lips split into a toothless grin. Ominous looking in his tattered shirt and filthy breeches, she debated calling for Lucian, but quickly set the thought aside when a cry of obvious pain sounded from the adjoining room.

"She is in here, Miss."

Constanza nodded and followed the man into the room. Almost spent, the woman winced in pain, despite being unconscious. Splayed out on the bed, the woman's spread legs revealed the gravity of the situation. The baby's head, crowning out the canal, threatened to suffocate the child, as the poor soul was fully dilated. A black tuft of hair was visible.

"How long has she been like this?"

"I reckon about a quarter hour. About a day in since her water broke."

"Are you a...relative?" she stammered.

"Um...no. A *friend* of the family."

"Where is the father?"

"There is no father. This child is illegitimate."

"Illegitimate or no, she did not impregnate herself! Where and whom is the father?"

"I would not be knowin' that, mum. Perhaps you can ask Delia...if she makes it that is." Toothless grinned maliciously.

She turned to call for Lucian when the woman revived, eyes wide, screaming out in pain.

"Oh please, please, mum. Help me. Help me save the baby, it will not come out!"

To her relief, the decrepit toothless wonder clicked the door shut. Stanzy placed her hands on either side of the infant's head, and with each undulating contraction gently inched the child along the birth canal. The woman's pelvis was inordinately small, and if she survived the birth of this child, Stanzy would advise her against trying to have any more children. She wasn't anatomically built for bearing children.

The baby reluctantly slid into the world in a rush of fluid and blood, drenching Stanzy's dress and boots. The infant lay still and quiet in her hands. Constanza turned him onto his stomach and smacked him square between the shoulder blades. Reaching inside his mouth, she swiped away the mucous. His tiny frame sputtered and coughed, finally renting the air with a loud wail.

She looked up to congratulate the mother, but the poor wretch was unconscious once again. Constanza turned the child over to examine him more fully, and what she saw made her blood run cold. The child's fingers, very long and pointed looked eerily familiar. Its fingernails were longer than normal as well. She shook the befuddlement away.

"It is a minor birth defect, nothing more," she said to what she thought was an empty room, "No worse than what is on my own hand."

"It is a changeling baby, I am sure of it," said the sans tooth harbinger. "We have been waiting for him to arrive!"

"*Lucian!*"

As they continued on to Nags Head in silence, Stanzy jumped when Lucian spoke loudly. "I am going to murder Hopkins for putting you in that dangerous situation. There is no way that woman was a business acquaintance of his. I am so sorry I did not go in with you!"

"It is all right, Lucian. I am alive, the baby is alive, and so is the mother. Although I am quite sure I do not wish to exchange places with her. No father, a disfigured child, and some sort of superstitious sailor as your chambermaid."

"What did he call the child?"

Constanza sighed. *How am I going to be able to forget what I have seen if Lucian insists on discussing it with me?*

"A changeling."

"What exactly is a changeling?"

She sighed again, reached into her mind and heard the fairies scratching at the door, anxious to tell their tales. "Changelings are known throughout Ireland as the children of fairies. They are usually abhorrent to look at, and as fairies are typically beautiful, legend says they steal human children and put their changeling babies in their stead."

Lucian looked at her intently, and his expression reminded her of Ben, staring animatedly during one of her lessons. She smiled into his rapt face.

"What?" he said perplexed.

"Nothing." She continued with her explanation of changelings. "After a few weeks, the babies' spines become hunched and they grow long, taloned fingers covered with hair and a full set of sharp pointy teeth. They usually do not live very long, only three or four years. Oh, yes—and they cry most of the day and night."

"Hmm...does not sound very pleasant." He didn't ask any further questions.

Propped against Lucian's shoulder, Stanzy felt sleep coming to claim her again. Eerie flute and fife music played in her head as she dreamt of every child she'd ever delivered with a birth defect.

The wagon hit a stone on the path, startling Constanza awake from her deep sleep. She was disoriented for a minute, until she felt Lucian's thigh under her head. Her soul swelled with unaccustomed feelings...comfort and relief. They were going to spend a week at Nags Head to celebrate their union with his Great Aunt Rose. All Lucian had told her about his aunt was that she was in sixty or so years out.

They'd also decided to wait until their trip home to visit Katrina in Bath. Perhaps she would want to return to StoneWater with them.

She could have lain in the back of the wagon, but she felt an indescribable urge to stay at his side. It was embarrassing to admit, as she'd always secretly laughed at women who were so taken with their husbands. Describing her previous views of love as cynical would be an understatement.

Closing her eyes again, she relished the feeling of security; knowing tomorrow it all could disappear. Take each good day for what it is.

Soon the wagon stopped. "Wake up, we are here."

A simple, but tasteful cottage sat near the surf line. Staring out onto the waves licking the beach, her breath caught in her chest.

She turned and caught Lucian eyeing her, then he looked back out to sea. "She can be beautiful, or she can be cruel as anything, like most women I know."

"I hope present company is excluded," Stanzy said, jabbing him in the ribs with her elbow.

Entering the kitchen of the cottage, a woman peered into a pot boiling on the stove. She turned to smile widely, and Stanzy thought she looked amazingly young for her age. Her graceful movements showed no sign of rheumatism or rigidity. Long, white hair streamed down her back past her shoulder blades, and she possessed the remnants of once great beauty.

"Aunt Rose!" Lucian bellowed, striding over and lifting the tiny woman off the ground in an embrace.

"Oh, my boy, it has been too long since you were here to visit your wizened old aunt!"

"Constanza, I would like you to meet my favorite aunt, Rose. Aunt Rose, this is my lovely wife, Constanza."

"It is a pleasure to finally meet you." Stanzy took the woman's hand. "I have heard so much about you."

"So you are the one who has captured my boy's heart so completely?"

Lucian turned puce, the color his skin reserved for his most mortifying moments.

"He is like no other," was all Stanzy could say.

Later, as they walked down the stretch of beach

holding hands, Lucian described the tides and the birds, and told her stories of the sea. Suddenly he dropped her hand and bolted down the beach toward something bobbing in the shallow surf. As he darted into the waves, he reminded her of a schoolboy who had been released to play in the water. He reached the object, picked it up in his hands and turned it over and over.

"Lucian, what are you doing?" she said breathlessly, running to see what had captured his attention so fully.

"Sorry. I thought it might be a piece of Ambergris."

"A what?"

"It is from the internal organs of Sperm whales. It has the finest oil, and is very dear. Perfume manufacturers will pay hugely for it! But it is not..."

He waded out of the water, his breeches wet up to his thighs.

"How is it you know so much of the sea, too, farmer?"

They sat on a dune and stared out at the white froth that tipped the incoming waves as they hit the shoreline, again and again.

"My father was on the lifesaving crews here. Because of the diamond shoals, shipwrecks are completely commonplace to us. There are groups of men to *this* day, who brave the swells in the hurricanes, to rescue stranded voyagers."

"Like you did for me..." She couldn't help but be amazed that she'd actually found someone so true and pure in motives. Unfortunately, she had come to believe people like Lucian didn't exist anymore, except in fairie stories her mother used to tell her as a child.

"Yes, but one night, when I was fourteen, during a particularly bad hurricane my father went out with the boats as he always did and did not return. He was lost to the sea that night. I had begged him to let me go with him as I felt I was old enough to help. I was so angry with him that he would not take me."

Constanza said nothing. She held very still and waited for him to continue.

It is so rare he opens up, I fear to even breathe lest

he quit speaking.

"My mother and I were left alone. I knew I would never be able to make my living at sea as my father had done. I could not stand to see it every day, and peer into its depths...wondering if he might be down there. My mother and I were hired at StoneWater—I to learn the fields and my mother as a servant to Mr. Kirkaldy. Mr. Kirkaldy and I were close as he never had any sons, and well, you can see what Sarah is like. She has not a whit of common sense and neither did her sisters. They were appalled when he wrote me into his will. He was a wonderful man who helped me countless times when he had no obligation to do so. Her father *worked* the land, and knew everything about it, unlike Ian. Anyway, I have long since forgiven my father. I look at Benjamin and know there is no way I would let him follow me out to sea at fourteen. He made the right decision. Otherwise, my mother would have been totally alone then."

She grabbed his hand and they sat in silence for a while.

On the way back to the cottage, when it was almost in sight on the horizon, he asked, "Tell me about your hand, Constanza."

She turned and put her face into the wind. The sun was setting now, and she didn't want to spoil this perfect day by reliving the memory. But he had given her something today—a piece of his past...of him. *How alike we are, carefully choosing our words and to whom we speak them.*

Guarded.

At peace with her decision, she sat atop a sand dune and very unladylike, hiked up her dress so she could sit cross legged.

Lucian slid beside her and quietly waited.

"It is quite simple really. I was fourteen and assisting my father in an amputation. Infection had set into the man's leg and I was holding his knee still, as Father sawed below the joint in an effort to salvage the rest of the leg. As usual, the lout had been drinking. I was not strong enough to use a bone saw, so I merely assisted.

In his inebriated state, Father slipped, quite unintentionally. I felt the pop before I felt any pain. Surprisingly, I did not feel *anything* for quite a while."

She sighed and permitted a few tears to fall, then faced her husband. "All right. That is only the second time I have ever told that story in its true form. I have fabricated every possible scenario to save face for my father."

He drew his gaze away from the shoreline and swallowed hard as he looked at her. "When was the first?"

"To my Uncle Delvin."

He leaned over and started to kiss her. "Thank you." His kisses became more urgent and he pulled her down between two sand dunes.

"What are you doing?"

"Constanza, we are married," he said as he continued to kiss her.

He stopped abruptly, and pulled back from her. His gaze stopped her and she waited.

"You can trust me. I will not hurt you. I am never letting you go."

"Even though I am wicked and stubborn? And completely unconventional?"

"Well, I have finally met my match, haven't I?"

"Are you sure you don't mind then?" Lucian, smiling like a fool, had nets and poles slung over his shoulder.

"Lucian, you have not left my side in three days. Go ahead and go, they won't wait much longer!"

From outside, two men waited. One yelled, "Lucian, some time before the new year! It is fishing, not leaving for battle!"

"Shut that door, boy, it is freezing out there!" chastised Rose.

Quickly stepping outside, he winked at Stanzy and pulled the door closed. Alone with his aunt for the first time, Constanza stared at the back of Rose's head, unsure what to say.

Rose turned and set a steaming mug of coffee in front of her. "You do like coffee, don't you?"

"I was raised on tea, but I have to admit I drink coffee more and more the longer I stay. So Rose, are you going to give me any tales of pirates? I hear so many of them now, I feel like I know some of them."

"Well, when you live down here on the island, The Brethren of the Coast are a somewhat necessary evil I am afraid."

"How so?"

"We are isolated here so we rely on goods brought in by boat. At times, the Brethren provide us with items we cannot get elsewhere."

Constanza nodded understanding. This woman was so practical it was like looking into a mirror. A spinster, Rose was self-sufficient and didn't require a man's support or care. Stanzy thought Rose the most clever woman she'd ever met.

"I have known many a merchant in Portsmouth to be more crooked than some of the Brethren."

"Really?" Stanzy sipped her coffee.

"Yes." Rose nodded, then changed the subject. "Many of us Bankers live well into our nineties. It must be something in the water on the island."

Constanza smiled broadly as she could see where Lucian had derived part of his personality.

"Rose, what was Lucian's first wife like? I hesitate to ask him about her—it just doesn't feel right somehow."

"Mae? She was a good girl and much like him—very forthright and kind."

"Were they happy?"

The woman stood and peered out the window. She gathered the shawl tighter as protection from the constant drafts seeping in around the windows.

"Yes, they were. She loved him very much, and he loved her. But I have to tell you, I have never seen him look at a woman the way he looks at you. You have obviously bewitched him."

"Well then, I guess I am under the same spell."

Rose laughed and nodded. "When he and his mother lost his father, they were quite *broken* for a long time, and I do not feel Lucian was ever quite whole again 'til he had Benjamin. It was like another side of his soul opened. Tell me, what was your family like?"

She shrugged. "Oh, you know, normal upbringing,"

Oh you liar! Amazing how lies still roll off my tongue when the situation demands it!

The afternoon wore on, and she awaited Lucian's return. Reclining on the chair by the fire, the sounds of Aunt Rose banging around in her kitchen were oddly comforting, the fire made her sleepy and warm.

She heard the office door tinkle its silver bell. Deep voices reverberated through the halls downstairs. She had no idea what was going on, as it was Sunday and her father didn't work on this day, except in dire emergencies.

She hadn't spoken to him for going on two weeks, except for the necessities of assisting in the office. Outside of direct commands, she had no communication with him. So she had no clue who might be visiting.

Her father no longer had any friends. The friends he'd managed to maintain while her mother was alive had drifted quietly away as he slid deeper and deeper into the bottle—leaving his children there to drown with him in the dregs.

Quietly tiptoeing down the stairs, she placed herself strategically outside his study door to listen.

"Well, there is no doubt of her beauty as I observed last week at the market. My only concern is her...disposition."

"How so? Please speak plainly."

"Your oldest daughter is attractive, but, well, you must admit highly irregular. Unconventional. I have seen her ride a horse to best my eldest son, and she works here with you."

Her father laughed cynically. "And she shoots a musket as well. I assure you, you will find none of that temperament with Katrina. She is concerned with the typical pursuits of ladies and has none of her sister's irregularities as you put it?"

Constanza sucked in her breath and peered through

the cracked door. The man was red faced and portly, but worst of all, as old as her father. Probably around sixty-two if she surmised correctly. And he intended to hand off Katrina—young, naive Katrina—to this man. No doubt for a heavy price.

Stealthily, she moved back up the stairs to the room where Katrina was fiddling with a piece of jewelry.

"Katrina, please, you need to leave NOW!"

"Whatever in the world are you talking about?"

"Downstairs, there is a man about father's age whom I believe wants to marry you."

"Oh! Is he handsome?"

Constanza gritted her teeth. "Look outside the window."

Her father and the older gent were lifting boxes out of the back of the carriage to bring inside.

"Oh my."

"Precisely. Run to the Inn and stay there until I come for you."

Tears welled in her sister's eyes, "Stanzy, what can you possibly do to stop him?"

"Leave that to me. Just go!"

Stanzy made her way down the staircase and met her father in the entryway.

"Constanza, this is Mr. Porterhouse. Could you go and fetch your sister for me?"

"I am afraid she has gone to market."

Her father's eyes narrowed. "I see." Then to his guest he said, "Well, it seems you and I will have to reschedule our meeting today." He began to lead Mr. Porterhouse back toward his carriage.

Constanza paced back and forth, awaiting his return. She knew this wouldn't go well.

For a moment she stood at the window looking out at the falling snow. She again fought the urge to run and free herself from this house, from him, from all this responsibility which weighed so heavily around her neck like a millstone.

She thought of what would happen to Will if she left. Visions of him going to the workhouse, or worse.

She closed her eyes tightly and prayed. It seemed it was all she did nowadays. Her hands began to shake and she opened and closed them, trying to control the tremors.

Her father reentered the house in a rage and flung open the door.

"Do not strike me again. You pathetic animal, you continue to hit me when I am a quarter of your size," she warned.

"Where did you send her? You knew, didn't you? We need the money, Constanza, if you expect to continue living under a roof. She is old enough to wed, and he has money to burn."

"He is your age, and drinks too much as well. I have seen him at the Inn, Father, and I know the likes of him. It was said he used to beat his first wife. As a matter of fact, it was rumored that he beat her to death. Because of his money and power, the charges were dismissed."

"Rubbish, all of it."

"You would sell your daughter, your own flesh and blood, on the chance this might be valid? You are a monster."

His speed took her by surprise as he crossed the room. As he cocked his fist, then struck her hard, it was as if she were watching the scene from another's point of view. A dream.

She didn't cower or cry out, but righted herself, and looked him directly in the eye. "I will go to Constable Englas and speak to him about your drinking. I will tell him you routinely operate and perform births while intoxicated."

Constable Englas had loved her mother all of her life, and Constanza as well as her father knew it. He was uncorrupt and would undoubtedly pursue the issue if brought to his attention.

"You wouldn't. Where would you go? What would you do?"

"Anywhere is better than here and anything is better than assisting a drunk. Oh and remember all of *my irregularities—I expect I can look after myself."*

He raised his hand to strike again, but something in her eyes stopped him. He stared at her. "Get out of my sight, you worthless child."

"Well, I am your daughter, aren't I? It would be difficult to be anything but worthless."

She started and sat bolt upright in the chair, only to see Aunt Rose staring at her from the other rocker, one eyebrow raised. "Nightmare?"

"No, I am fine, really."

"Constanza, is your father still alive?"

"Why do you ask?"

You were saying, "Father...over and over again."

~ *Chapter Nine* ~

The days in Nags Head passed like a dream to Constanza. Never had she felt so welcomed, despite being a stranger to these people. Bankers were all (well most, every town has its loons) helpful and kind, and as Rose had said, lived to an extraordinary number of years. Stanzy's medical brain told her it must be their diet, but her adventurous brain questioned if the place might be enchanted. Fantastic stories about the place abounded, as their trips to the beach or people's homes attested.

Storytelling was a profession in the Banks. Each night one person tried to outdo another with some spectacular tale of pirates, the sea or a local mystery.

Constanza was officially warned that into the drink she would go, if she couldn't produce a tale soon. Not usually a creative sort, she felt tonight would be the night the sea would call her name if she didn't come up with a yarn to spin.

Lucian squeezed her hand gently as they walked to the roaring fire on the beach. Thirty or so of Lucian's friends sat laughing and drinking. Once they spotted Lucian and Stanzy, countless handshakes and cries of "Lucian, old man! Where have you been?" and "How did you manage to get *her* to marry *you!*" began.

Two stories unfolded and the bravado and wordplay kept her on the edge of her seat until the teller had concluded. Constanza then permitted herself to exhale as the excitement concluded.

Jon, the undeclared master of ceremonies, turned to her. "Come now, Constanza. England is the home to many famous writers—surely you have *one* story for us!"

"I am not a storyteller by nature. My mother had a gift for it. Give me a moment and I will give it a go."

Concentrate, she told herself. She stared off into the waves for a few moments, while the quiet sounds of people laughing and fire crackling filled her unconscious hearing. She pictured her mother sitting by the hearth in her rocking chair, needlepoint in hand as she attempted to keep her two daughters entertained and complete her work at the same time.

Maura Smythe's soothing voice filled Constanza's ears, and her eyes welled up with tears at the wonderful memory of a time when she'd felt protected.

"I have thought of one," she proclaimed boldly to the group.

All eyes turned to her. Lucian's hand slipped behind her back in reassurance. He didn't look at her, but his touch let her know she could be herself here without reservation.

"My dear mother was from Ireland, and she always had a story to tell. Not sweet ones of maids and princes, however. But tales where it seemed she wanted to scare the knickers off of us."

This brought an appreciative round of chuckling from the circle and Constanza relaxed a bit.

"This is one she told on a cold, windy night. The Moruadh are creatures from the land of Tir fo Thoinn, or the land beneath the waves. They resemble beautiful women, but are not destined to walk the lands surrounding the seas. One day, a man from Cork was strolling along the shoreline near his home when he happened upon a beautiful green cloak hidden in the thicket by his cottage. Behind him, sounded a strange voice. It resembled a gull shrieking and the call of a humpback whale, mingled together.

"Turning, he saw a woman. Long, blonde hair, stringed with seaweed, obscured her face. She stood taller than he at six feet and was naked as the day she was born.

"At the sight of him, she began to cry so he took her into his home. Once the hair and seaweed were cleared from her face, he beheld the most beautiful woman he'd ever seen. So beautiful was she that, despite being a principled man, he felt compelled to lie with her. And he did so the very instant she stepped over the threshold into his cottage. She became pregnant and reluctantly agreed to become his bride.

"Over the years, the Corker noticed certain traits his wife possessed that immensely troubled him. One was that she did not often speak, for which he was sure some husbands would be grateful—"

Several snickers erupted amongst the listeners, then immediately quieted as Stanzy continued.

"But when she finally did speak her voice had an odd sing-song quality that made him feel stupid and sleepy.

"Another thing was that her feet were webbed. And, as if that were not troubling enough, two of their four children also had the webbing. He tried to tell himself this was just an oddity and he should not spit good fortune in the eye.

"Still, other problems pricked his conscience. Each and every night she would stare out at the sea, and when she did this her face would resemble one mooning over a lost lover.

"On several occasions, he caught her frolicking in the waves at night. When he approached the water he saw fins moving around her and splashes within feet of her, which quickly disappeared into the blackness when they sensed his presence. He tried not to let it bother him, as he felt she was only truly happy when in the sea. Also, it was the only time she smiled, which was fine with the Corker as her teeth were a little too pointed for his liking.

"One day, as her husband watched, she opened an old trunk and was surprised as she gazed upon the cloak she'd lost the day she'd met her husband. She picked it up and caressed it lovingly against her cheeks. Slowly, her hair began to lose its blonde luster. It changed before her frightened husband and children's eyes to the color of seaweed."

Purposefully, Stanzy paused, letting the tension

build. She gazed around at the expectant faces, putting a slight look of apprehension on her face. Then she continued.

"She slipped on the cloak, and walked out the door of the cottage to the water's edge. She only looked back one time as she waded into the surf, and when she opened her mouth to utter a parting farewell, the shrieks of a seagull rent through the morning salt air.

"Creatures of all types filled the waves to congratulate her on her return to the surf, and she then returned to Tir fo Thoinn.

"So it is the wisest course, that if one lives by the sea, to make sure and check the feet of the bride, before she slips on her wedding shoes."

The circle of Bankers was quiet after she stopped speaking. Amused, Stanzy saw several of the younger men in the group sneak glances at their girlfriend's feet, which were buried in the sand by the glowing fire.

Applause for the tale began all at once, with a few shouting "More!"

Lucian turned to smile at her.

Over the next few days Stanzy felt more at ease and accepted than she ever had in her life. Dining at neighbor's homes each evening, she found the people were unassuming and kind.

Later in the evening, Aunt Rose would be hosting a gathering as their visit was winding to a close.

Guests sat around the fireplace, while outside, the night wind whipped around ferociously. Those of Lucian's close friends who were married brought their wives, so the party in the small cottage numbered fourteen.

Andrew walked to the window and peered out at the surf. "It is shaping into a right storm tonight!"

The six men present nodded in agreement and Lucian strode to Andrew's side. "And it is a cold one out there."

"How cold will it get?" Constanza asked.

Andrew looked serious for a moment before replying, "There's been times when a wreck off the coast could not be reached, and the men froze solid to the rigging."

"Andrew! Constanza has no use for tales such as that I am sure!" chastised Virginia, his wife.

Amused, Lucian said, "She is a rare breed of woman. I expect she would man the boats if she were a stronger swimmer."

A bell sounded outside and Stanzy watched the women's faces drain of color.

"What is that?" she asked quickly.

Directing his attention to her, Lucian said, "The lifesaving station bell. There must be trouble in the water."

In unison, the men began to gather their belongings in a practiced, orderly manner.

Virginia cast a concerned look at her husband. "I will go and pick up little Andy and meet you at home when...it's over."

As people exited the cottage, Lucian gently pulled Constanza into the kitchen and hugged her tightly to him. "I will be especially careful, but I must go with them."

"I understand." She would expect no less of him, or herself.

After Lucian left, Constanza sat staring at the fire as Aunt Rose steadily rocked in her chair on the hearth rug. She checked the time again—only one hour since he had departed, but it felt like a year.

Sympathetically, Rose said, "I know child, waiting is always more difficult than anything else. Be glad you do not live so close to the shore year round, as you would have to endure this often. Lucian's mother had to. The boy is steadfast."

"That is an understatement," Stanzy said offhanded-ly, and a little too curtly.

Time passed, and neither spoke as Stanzy paced back and forth across the room. Suddenly, the silence wore on her and she realized she may have offended her new in-law.

She walked and stood in front of Rose. "I apologize.

I admit I do not know what to do with myself. I have never been the waiting at home sort."

The old woman smiled. "No. You, too, are steadfast."

Stanzy laughed out loud, "Yes, I am. I am just as stubborn as he is."

"Us Bankers do not have time for the petty emotions mainlanders express. For a goodly long time, just to keep alive from the elements, we had to band together. So we wish each other well, and are there for one another. It is necessary for our survival."

"Yes. I know. Many persons I have been acquainted with over my lifetime are a jealous sort. When something good happens to others they feign happiness, but it always shows in their eyes that they truly do not mean it. I think one has to know oneself and be comfortable with who we are, in order to not let the ugly side of the emotions come through."

"It also has to do with what life has shown you. If you see enough suffering, you learn to appreciate what is important," said Rose quietly. "Must have been too many whales killed this year."

"Pardon?"

"You mean Lucian never told you that in years when too many whales and dolphins are killed, it means we will have many storms?"

Constanza shook her head in disbelief. "I cannot wait any longer...where should I go?"

Stanzy took the covered wagon and headed south to the surf area Aunt Rose had described. She'd a lit lantern beside her and futilely tried to see into the gale. Although not a hurricane, it was a nasty storm nonetheless.

Farther down the coast, she spied something—a huge black mass in the water.

She arrived in time to see the last longboat team hit the massive swells. As they cut across diagonally, the boat crested high on a wave then crashed down the same distance. Stanzy became nauseated just watching it.

Running down onto the beach, she stopped in the shallow water.

What do you think you are doing? You are not a strong swimmer. Be sensible, stay put. Before long the boats will bring passengers alive to shore. Then you can assist.

A massive explosion rocked the night sky. In the fiery glow, longboats could be seen in the water around the wreckage. An involuntary gasp escaped her throat, and her hands flew to cover her mouth. The light from the blaze showed men, women and children, leaping from the partially capsized vessel into the churning sea.

The first rescue longboat was making its way to shore when a massive swell caught and held it suspended for what seemed an eternity before it overturned. Lightning lit the sky grotesquely, allowing Constanza to watch the shapes slip into the inky water. Thunder boomed and she jumped at the sound.

She began to run, pulling her dress over her head and tossing it aside as she headed into the water. Its weight would pull her under. Visions from dreams of women sinking to the bottom, while they struggled to release themselves from the heavy materials surrounding them, filled her head.

Clad only in her shift, Constanza plunged into the surf, heading toward the capsized vessel. She dove again and again, frantically feeling all around her for anything that felt human. Finally, her hand grabbed what she thought was seaweed, but nonetheless she pulled it up with all her might. Clutched in her fist was a handful of hair—a little girl floated limp and lifeless.

She fought the waves pounding the shoreline and carried the child up to the wagon, placing her in the back on her side. Quickly, she wrapped a blanket around her and pounded furiously on her back. In no time, the girl vomited seawater and ragged breathing commenced. Pulling the cover tighter around her, Stanzy cautioned her to stay put.

Racing to the shore again, Stanzy stopped short.

A woman was dazedly searching through the surf.

Repeatedly she went down and scrambled up again. Stanzy watched her spew out seawater and scream from her fallen position. "Ella! Ella! Where are you?"

Constanza helped her stand, grabbed her by the shoulders and shook her. The woman was in shock. "Is Ella blonde?" Stanzy yelled over the wind and pounding surf.

The woman looked at her, trying to comprehend the question. Then she screamed, "Yes!"

"She is safe, in the wagon, up there." Stanzy pointed.

The woman lumbered forward, falling in the sand, then regained her posture. Stanzy saw her reach the wagon.

Longboats were arriving on shore in droves now. At least twelve by her count, all with screaming people and a few animals.

A huge explosion resounded through the night air. Constanza looked out to the wreck just in time to see it disappear below the waterline.

Another ship for the Atlantic graveyard.

Stanzy ran to the wagon, removed blankets and began to meet the injured on the beach, helping them to the wagon. All the while her stomach clenched tighter and tighter.

Where is he?

Where is he?

Please, I am not sure I can continue to breathe if he does not come back. Why did I ever fall in love?

She'd put the first stitch into a gash in a young man's arm when she felt thick arms encircle her waist. A voice in her ear whispered, "What a grand holiday I have brought you on, my darling!"

"Oh, thank You, God," she cried, as she turned and flung her arms around his neck.

Fingers traced the musket on her lap as they headed toward Bath to find Katrina. Stanzy's troubled mind raced.

Aunt Rose had made them promise a return visit soon after the baby was born. Every time Constanza insisted she wasn't pregnant, Rose just gave her a knowing look.

Surely with my background, I would know.

Her head bobbed and dipped as the rattle and movement of the carriage lulled her to sleep after the night's toiling against the storm.

"Come here, Constanza." Uncle Delvin's deep rumbling baritone beckoned. His formidable voice completely contradicted his personality, for he was the most approachable man she'd ever met, not to mention the only one she'd ever felt truly loved her. Hands so massive, his fingers looked like little bangers to her as a child.

"Yes, Uncle?" She didn't feel the day could have gotten any better. He'd come and taken her by herself to the country. He had let her ride one of his new, best horses. His cook served her supper, and as she was usually the one doing the serving, it was a fantastic treat.

It wasn't very often that anyone was concerned with her happiness, so this special time was utopia in her eyes.

"I want to teach you something today, and I want you to keep it between us—a secret if you will. Not many people would approve of it as it is entirely unconventional for a lady, but let's face it poppet, nothing in your sixteen years has been conventional."

He pulled out his musket and handed it to her. When she took it, her hands fell a few inches with the weight.

"I will not always be around to look after you, and your brother and sister. I will sleep better knowing you are able to defend yourself." He removed the powder horn.

She swallowed hard and studied every movement as he poured the gunpowder into the barrel.

"You need a piece of cloth, as a seal over the gunpowder." He ripped off a small scrap from a larger cloth and spat on it. "This is called a spit patch."

Her eyes narrowed. He rolled his eyes and said, "It is to create a seal for pressure in the barrel. My goodness child, that mind was made for science."

He handed her the lead ball. "Place it in the barrel and then use your 'rod' to push it down. You must make sure it is all the way down to the powder. Once your rod bounces a bit when you drop it, then you know it is ready."

She cocked the gun, and he poured the powder into the frism pan. "Make sure some powder gets into the hole, so that the ignition spark travels inside."

As she shot the musket the first time, the noise made her jump. By the end of the day, she was able to use the sights to at least shoot in a general direction. As night began to fall Uncle Delvin helped her into the carriage, and she found herself wishing she could stay with him—forever. When she was here, she actually felt a little like a child again, as she knew he would take care of her.

But it was not to be. As they approached Bristol, the tears started to streak down her filthy face, cutting black tracks on her cheeks. Although she loved her siblings dearly, she dreaded returning to this life.

He put his arm around her. "I know how it is for you, but I am out to sea most of the year, and he is still your father. I will be back as soon as I am able, and I will bring all of you out to my manor, for a fortnight next time."

As they rattled along on the way to Hawthorne House, Stanzy's thoughts kept returning to Aunt Rose, and her striking personality. During their time together, Stanzy had learned, much to her delight, that Rose had knowledge of healing maladies using nutrients from the sea. It seemed like another lifetime since her mother had shared the herbal teachings with her.

Rose told her she'd discovered oil from cod had healing properties that dramatically aided vision in some of the older folks. She'd been cautioned by other Bankers, however, just to use the oil from the fish, and not the fish's liver, as some had died when this was used.

Constanza immediately thought of Megan's photophobia. Something was clearly wrong with the child's eyes, for she continually squinted, or looked out of the corner of her eye at you. Occasionally Megan would take shiny objects and whisk them back and forth across her field of vision and scream with delight. Other days, she could barely open her eyes.

Stanzy was anxious to try this treatment on her, which she decided must be absolutely better than leeches.

Katrina almost took flight, bounding off the porch steps of Hawthorne House.

She flung herself around Constanza's neck. Stanzy reluctantly admitted she'd rarely seen Katrina look so well. Her dark brown hair curled around her face and her cheeks flushed with happiness.

"Oh, I am so glad to see you, Mrs. Smythe!" she bubbled. "And you, Lucian. Oh, I forgot, Mrs. Blackwell!"

They sat sipping tea in the sitting room. The master and mistress of the house frequently traveled, leaving the care of the children to Katrina.

"It has been glorious here. The children complete their studies and then I am free to do as I please. I have had so many gentlemen callers since I arrived, I can barely count them all! I have two that I favor, one is named Anthony Thomason, and I am afraid you quite know the other well—dear Edward."

"Teache?" sputtered Lucian, losing half the mouthful of tea back into his cup. "Katrina, you can't be serious."

Her eyes narrowed. "Oh, I am deadly serious, dear brother. Although Anthony is beautiful to look at, I am afraid he is poor as a church mouse. Edward, on the other hand...well let's just say he can provide me with the means to a secure life. Look, he brought me back this from his last voyage."

Around her neck was a beautiful gem of unrecognizable origin to Stanzy. She looked gravely at Lucian from behind Katrina's back when she turned to address him.

Constanza took a deep breath before speaking and silently said a prayer so that she might be articulate and reach Katrina's heart with her meaning. She knew deep down, however, that as much as you might love someone, you cannot change *inherently who they are*. So, even as she spoke the words, she was certain they would fall on deaf ears.

"Katrina, darling. I understand the practicality of marrying into a more favorable station and arrangement. You know that I am nothing if not pragmatic. But, one must be sure of the character of the betrothed, because if the character is heavily flawed, then the amount of heartache will far outweigh any benefits of a comfortable living."

Lucian held very still, not commenting on what she'd just spoken. She caught the briefest twitch under his eye.

Here it comes...

"Oh! I should have known you could not just be happy for me! Just because he did not meet *your* high standards, does not mean he is not worth considering as a match! You are jealous of me! You always have been." Katrina leaped off the settee and set to pacing back and forth in front of Constanza, her hands balled into fists.

Jealous of what? Your oblivion of all things necessary? That I cannot live in your dream world? Maybe I am jealous of that!

Inhaling deeply, Constanza exerted a level of self-control she saved exclusively for Katrina and Will. By the look on Lucian's face, he was clearly amazed she'd held her temper in check. Probably thinking she wouldn't have hesitated to unleash an onslaught of words on him had he acted like Katrina.

He stood. "Ladies, I am going to take a turn on the grounds."

After he departed, Constanza grabbed her sister's hand. "Kitty, I am not jealous. I only want what is best for you. Yes, I would have you marry so that you were secure, but also for love. If the young man you described has not taken your heart, then perhaps neither of these suitors is right for you. Let us be honest, you are beautiful and intelligent. Many more offers will be made to you."

"You do not understand, Stanzy. I want out of here. I cannot stand being a governess! I have no other profession that is more favorable, however. If I marry Edward, I can leave here, and have servants of my own."

Stanzy tried to think quickly, how to make someone so young see that the easy decision was rarely the correct one? That having a marriage with who knows what horrible toils, would hardly be worth having servants?

"Katrina, I know you are not going to believe me, but nothing ever worth doing is easy—there may be a few exceptions, but it is usually true. Marrying Edward would be easy, and a quick answer to a problem you have, but over the course of time, I am certain a much more favorable alternative will present itself. Have patience. Have faith."

At this, Katrina managed a real smile. "Dearest Stanzy. You have always been the one with all the patience. When we were children, you were the one who could wait for dessert, and wait to open a present 'til everyone else had done so first. I think mother gave you all of the patience, and had none left to give me when I came along. Please stay a few days. Edward is to return soon, and I would love for you and Lucian to sup with us."

Stanzy conjured this picture in her mind and almost laughed out loud. The recollection of Lucian with his pistol pointed at Teache's head, firmly fixed in her mind.

"Katrina, that would not be a good idea. I would love to meet your other suitor, however."

As Hawthorne House receded from view, Constanza glared over her shoulder at it.

That was a waste of time and effort. I feel worse than I did before. With all the foolish decisions she is making, I fear she may turn into our father with a 'poof' at any time.

Remorse sickened her gut at having spent half her life trying to keep her sister safe and alive, and now as an adult, Katrina was putting herself in jeopardy. At times like these, she actually wished for a magic wand that could return Katrina to a child. True things were awful then, but at least she knew her whereabouts and that she was safe.

Lucian looked at Constanza's somber face. "Well, Anthony was quite a good fellow," he said hopefully.

"Yes. Unfortunately, a lot of good that will do, since he is not Edward Teache."

Opening her eyes, the child's breath came in gasps. She stood on tiptoes and craned her neck to see out the carriage window. Immediately she recognized the dark old stones, the chimneys with smoke billowing out of them. Her tiny hands shook with the memories, and what would come next inside that wretched building.

Unable to stop them, the screams flew out of Megan's mouth.

~ *Chapter Ten* ~

She lay curled on the cot on the dirt floor. Shaking from the cold, Megan fingered the rough horse blanket. No one else had come in; she was alone. She didn't like alone. But if the others came, they would scare her. Big like Ma and Pa, they didn't act like them.

The *others* pulled her hair and hit her and pushed her off the cot at night.

She didn't understand why she was so different. Even in little ways. Like Ma and Bess could wear dresses, but when she put one on, her skin came alive, as if bugs crawled all over her. And the pain in her head—it was so great at times, the only way to stop it was to hit it, or push it against something hard.

She could learn some things. Like she'd been taught biting and kicking, they were wrong. But silly things made her so mad, almost everyday, and then she had no control of how she acted.

She so wanted to be good.

They would come for her, wouldn't they? Ma and Pa wouldn't forget about her and leave her here. She could not tell them what she wanted, the words...they just stayed up there...stuck in her head, which was why she got so angry. Except lately Ma had taught her a way to make her mouth speak, and even her body to do what she told it to do. And then this speaking with her fingers.

Megan, signed *Help* and then *Stop*. Bess had said it was a miracle. Whatever a miracle was she knew she liked it.

When she thought *Run* she could run! It was the best few days ever; until one of the men from the

Blackhouse came and made her cry. Since then, she hadn't been able to get her body to listen to her.

She didn't know if she would live if they put her in the cold bath like last time.

Suddenly, an old woman was in the cell—pitched in by a pair of hands it almost looked like she'd flown in. The woman fell in a heap onto the floor in front of her. For a while, she just lay there. Then the woman spoke in a funny voice, like the one Ma made sometimes when she read scary stories.

"Who is there? Who is here with me? Is it you, Mary?"

On her hands and knees, the old woman started crawling toward Megan. Her bony fingertips brushed the end of Megan's boot. She pulled away as if she'd been bitten.

"Who is that? Come closer so that I may see you."

Quick as she knew how Megan scrambled to the corner of the cell, closed her eyes and began to rock back and forth, staying in a safe place in her mind.

In her mind's eye, the swing behind home came into view. The grass was green and the boys were there. She felt their hands on her back as they pushed her on the swing. She wanted her soft doll, and the way Ma swung her round and round. Tears came from her eyes, which she hated because every drop burned her cheek like she'd been scratched.

Hearing more noise, she opened her eyes. A *young* 'other' was thrown into the room and sprawled onto the floor beside the old one.

"Mary, is that you?" old one said as she moved closer to the new young one, whose hair was matted and so long it hung below her bottom.

"No, you old caw!" younger said, swinging at the old one's head.

Then on their knees, they locked arms and pushed each other until they were quickly rolling on the dirt. Barely missing Megan, she realized they were fighting. This time she not only closed her eyes, but covered her ears as well.

Some sounds, like a baby crying or a dog barking, made her feel like someone was driving a stake into her head.

Like now. The old one howled like a wolf.

She tried not to cry, because then they would take notice of her, and the young one might attack her instead of the old woman.

She filled her mind with Ma and Bess, and her puppy. They *had* given her one, just like the boys. No one thought she noticed, because she couldn't speak, but she would look out her window and see the boys with their dogs, and wished she could try to run with the dogs as they did.

Now, the young one sat atop the old one. She held her arms down on the floor. Younger was pulling older's eyebrow hairs out a few at a time while the wolf-woman howled.

Megan stared. Were her eyes seeing right? Younger had no eyelashes or eyebrows. Seemed she ran out of her own, and decided to now pull out wolf-woman's instead.

With this howl, some of *the men* came in.

One man grabbed the young one. She kicked out her legs and her teeth bared like a nasty dog from home. Megan peeked long enough to see younger bite down into his arm, and now it was the man's turn to scream. Two other men ran in. One man held younger's arms across her chest in a criss-cross. She struggled, hanging in the air between the two while a third man grabbed her kicking feet. Carrying her off through the doorway, she arched her back and banged her head—hard—off the door. Megan thought she must have given up because her body went limp.

The old one cried. Megan tilted her head in wonderment. A minute ago they were fighting, now old one was sad. Old one picked up a doll that looked like Megan's favorite one at home. She sat in the middle of the dirty floor, rocking back and forth, repeating over and over, "Mary, my Mary."

Megan could hold her own sadness inside no longer,

her wailing filled the room and echoed through the cell.

The man's head shot in her direction and his eyes narrowed. Had he forgotten she was here?

Walking over, he picked her up. Megan didn't resist. She was at their mercy. He carried her down the hall and yelled to a woman, "All right, this wee one has to get out of there, lest the wicked sisters kill her for certain."

Megan paced, her feet making sounds off the walls as she stamped on the cold hard floor. She had her own room, so at least it was quiet.

Then *the men* had taken her to the *food place*. While there, the two big men had begun to fight and they were on the ground rolling. Many of the *Blackhouse* white coats jumped in and tried to separate them.

That was when she'd done it—she slipped out the door.

I have to find a way out. A way home.

Now she walked the hallways, passing each door, eyeing the people inside each room.

Door one: Tied to a chair, a crooked man sat staring out the window.

Door two: Arms lifted high in the air, a beautiful woman with grey hair down to her knees twirled as if dancing with someone only she could see.

Door three: A girl maybe her own age chewed at ropes tied to her wrists. When the young girl spied her, she started to scream.

Megan ran.

She ran until she couldn't hear the screams anymore. Scared...she was so scared. Finally, the fear started to go away and she realized she'd run up the stairs to the next floor.

Slowly she walked, watching all the while for white coats, and the *monsters* inside of them.

Then she started running again, bent over from fear. She heard noises that meant the *Blackhouse Men* were looking for her. Opening a door she stared at steps. She climbed to the top level of the *Blackhouse*. There were no more stairs.

This floor was wet. Looking up she saw holes in the roof. Why were holes up there? Water dripped from the holes and filled the hallways. The steady drip, drip, drip, made her shiver as she remembered the baths here. She looked in each room as she passed, searching for somewhere safe to hide.

A *clomp* at the end of the hallway caused her to freeze. She saw movement as something passed into the hallway from one of the rooms. She opened a closet and closed the door behind her, willing herself still.

Something whisked past the bottom of her skirt and she clapped her hands to her mouth to keep from screaming. *Just rats, just rats*, her mind repeated. They are better than *the bugs* or the *cold water*.

Then she heard the housemaid pull a bucket past the door. The woman whistled a strange tune Megan thought she'd heard once. Tilting her head to the side she closed her eyes, trying to recall the song.

The door to the stairwell opened and closed. The whistling went slowly away.

Carefully she opened the door, peeked left and right down the hall. No humans in sight. She leapt her way across the puddles in search of a safe place. Some of the rooms looked awful and she didn't even want to step into them; she hoped *no one* ever had to go into them. She found a candle and lit it, a skill she'd learned by watching Bess.

Holding it up, she peered into the gloom. Many mattresses were now the homes of families of rats, their eyes gleaming in the candlelight as it shone on their shiny black bodies. She shivered.

She continued down the hall, finally finding a room that seemed to be animal free. At the window she stood, seeing for miles over the beautiful grounds.

If not for the woods, it would look like a garden... but these woods are not like those at home.

Gathering blankets she'd found for warmth, she relaxed and her mind began to drift to home.

She thought of Mother. Not the mother that was small and had the pinched face and wrinkled nose. That wasn't a mother.

At night, when everyone thought her asleep, she would often look at the picture books in her room. Several contained pictures of women in rocking chairs, holding children close, reading to them from books.

THAT was a *mother*. She just knew it was.

No matter what anyone else said, the one they called Stanzy—she was Mother. She wanted so much to see her now. Mother would often hold her on her lap and whisper words...words she didn't understand, but by *how* she spoke them to her, she knew they must mean something good.

I want to go home, I want to go home. Please let me go home.

Megan cried again, but more softly this time. She drew her legs up to her chest and began to rock. Finally she fell asleep.

She awoke to dogs barking.

Close.

Shaking her head to clear it, she listened—her one sense that worked *really* well. Tree branches scratched the window. Was a storm coming? A single cricket chirped outside. Now...now she heard dogs clawing at the floors below in search of her.

Scared, she searched for an escape. She saw something she recognized from home. She walked over to it and eased open its hatch. Dishes and glasses were still inside, so she quietly pushed them aside just enough to squeeze her body in. The dumbwaiter slowly began to rumble down, but it squeaked noisily.

She could hear the dogs' barking move away as she felt herself falling farther and farther down.

At last it hit the bottom with a thump, and she sat...listening. No sounds—she cracked the door open a little.

What she saw next made her close her eyes and rub them vigorously. Surely she must be having a nightmare.

In a room filled with beds and comfortable looking chairs, unlike any she'd seen before in the *Blackhouse,* sat human statues. Climbing out of the dumbwaiter, she slowly began to walk through the room, fearing if she moved too quickly it might awaken them. And who knew what they would do—perhaps claw at her.

One beautiful woman with black hair sat in a chair at the window, her back straight, an arm raised, her head tilted to the right—posed as if listening. Megan moved around to the front of the chair and stared intently into her face. The woman stared unblinking. In a brief flash, she wondered if this were how she looked to others when she crawled into her mind.

She waved her hand in front of the woman's face, but the breathtaking statue didn't stir or blink. Her fingernails had grown so long they curled from each finger.

An old man sat on a chair with both arms raised to the heavens. The man's head and neck were so tilted that Megan looked up to see if the answer might be on the ceiling. A feeling she didn't like raced down her spine and she stepped back.

It seemed people could act like this no matter what age or whether a man or a woman.

An older woman lay curled on a bed like a baby. Megan got closer and was tempted to touch her to see if she still drew breath, but she couldn't make herself do it.

Scratching on the floor overhead awakened her to the current danger. They were coming.

She bolted as quickly as her legs would carry her into the hall and ducked into another room.

Where am I? Where are all the people who act like Ma and Pa? Why do they act like they cannot see me? Have I disappeared? She reached down and patted herself all over to make sure she was still solid.

In the next room all the people moved, but they looked really strange.

Everywhere her eyes beheld old women—all holding dolls in their arms. Several stood in a circle, their weight shifting back and forth in unison, as one sang a lullaby. Others sat in rocking chairs, cradling the dolls to their bosoms and whispering sounds to babies that weren't real.

The room was filled with a blend of whispering and lullabies at a pitch that made Megan's ears sting in pain. Covering her ears, she shook her head back and forth, losing touch with reality for a moment. This happened to her when her world became too loud or too bright or too much of anything.

I cannot stand the noise. It hurts my ears. It hurts too much.

She fought the urge to leave and crawl inside herself, but she knew if she did, they would find her and things would be much worse.

She willed her legs to move, but they stayed rooted to the spot. Her mind was too focused on blocking out the sounds for her to move her legs.

"Stop it!" she finally yelled and all the old eyes instantly turned to her.

The sounds ceased and, as if by magic, her legs were freed. She fled as one woman reached for her, but missed.

They are near. If they find me, it is back into the water or worse. The barking dogs were so close she could hear them sniffing.

She reached a room that had a strange rope arrangement across it that reminded her of a spider web. Small enough, she easily slid under one of the gaps in the ropes.

The people in this room wandered. A man walked in circles over and over again, never stepping off his unseen path.

A young woman opened and closed, opened and closed a door.

A young man sat and hummed to himself as he continually watched a music box spin.

She hid behind one of the rockers, and held her breath.

"Where could she be? We have searched every one of the floors, four times over."

"Heads will roll if she is not found! Continue the search!"

Two men in white jackets peered into the *repetition room*, the candles they held making their faces look scary.

Megan sat as still as one of the statue people until their lights faded to darkness.

She lay down on her side in the room and curled into a ball. Somehow she wasn't frightened in here. She didn't believe these people would even notice her.

Megan waited for what seemed like hours. Sneaking out of the repetition room, she headed up the staircase to the next floor. The dumbwaiter had carried her almost to the basement level of the *Blackhouse*.

This floor was decidedly colder, and she saw no one. Most of the rooms she passed were empty. In a few, older people were lying in beds—they appeared to be sleeping.

At the end of the hallway, she saw a door that had a rope net over it to keep the occupant inside. Looking up, she saw at the very top of the door, a small space between the net and the ceiling. Inside the room a woman sat rocking, softly humming a haunting tune. Her room was different from the others. Pictures hung all over her walls, and she even had a beautiful polished tea set.

Stomach rumbling, Megan looked hungrily at the tea tray. They hadn't let her eat anything for two days. Since the forced vomiting, her stomach made noise almost continually. In the silence, the sound was truly loud.

The woman must have heard for she turned and looked at Megan. Smiling, the woman beckoned to her.

Megan realized she remembered this woman from the last time she'd been here, only then the lady had eaten with everyone else. She'd given Megan part of her food and held her on her lap. The only five minutes of her last *visit* that she'd felt safe had been in this woman's arms.

"Sadie! Oh Sadie! I was wondering where you had gotten to! Come in. Why, I have cookies you can have."

Megan looked the rope net up and down and then at the cookies by the tea. With ease, she climbed the ropes and reached the space between ceiling and door. She contorted her torso until she was parallel with the ground and squeezed her way in. Throwing her legs over, she came down the other side, and landed with a *thud* at the woman's feet.

Happily clapping, the woman opened her arms.

Megan crawled over, let the woman squeeze her, and tried not to sob.

"Come sit, darling, you must be starving!"

She tried to chew, cry and nod as she crammed cookies into her mouth

"Sadie! Is that the manners I taught you?"

Voices could be heard and footsteps clomping along the hallways.

"Check in Sonata's room."

"How could she get in there?"

Megan shook her head back and forth.

The old woman looked at her and toward the sound of the voices "You must hide. *They* are coming for you."

She walked toward her open window, which was slightly cracked and tried to heave it up. Unable to raise it higher, Megan rushed to her side to help. It only budged a few inches more, but it was enough for Megan to slide her body out onto the ledge.

The voices were now inside Sonata's room. Megan began to inch along the ledge.

"She is outside on the sill! If she is killed, heads will roll. Her family is wealthy."

"Don't you touch Sadie!" Megan heard the kind woman shout over the noise of voices.

In the courtyard, many patients out for their daily exercise in the fenced courtyard stopped to stare up at her. They looked as if they had been frozen in time.

She struggled to crawl up the sloping roof, to an open window where she could get back into the *Blackhouse.*

A man at the window looked into her eyes and smiled. No kindness was in his smile, something closer to madness. On all fours he came out the window and slowly scaled the roof toward Megan. His feet slipped and he grabbed at the roof, searching for a hold. Fearful, Megan stood still. Then he suddenly leapt toward her, hands flailing wildly in the air in an attempt to grab her.

She dodged and his lunge was rewarded with a fistful of her shift.

The man tottered in place and lost his footing. His body aimed for the ground as he hurdled down the roof, pulling her with him. She screamed along with Sonata who was screaming from inside.

"Let me go!" she finally managed to get out. His face registered shock and amazement to hear her speak. He let her go seconds before he lost contact with the roof and began his free fall.

A sickening thud echoed below.

Megan buried her face in her hands and crawled back to the place in her mind from whence she'd come.

"How is it, pray tell, that a child the age of five is able to outsmart fifteen orderlies, and sends one plummeting to his death?" Dr. Vorhath spoke through clenched teeth as he pounded his fist against the massive table.

"Sir, the child *is* intelligent—capable of reasoning and problem solving."

"Nonsense! She is little more than an animal, with no feeling or awareness of anything except her most primitive instincts."

"We have her in solitary confinement, sir."

"And there she will stay 'til I decide what else should be done to improve her mind."

Megan rocked in the dark.

She opened her eyes, closed her eyes, but it all looked the same. She began to crawl on her hands and knees around the floor, tracing the room's outline.

Where am I? What have they done with the light? Where are Ma and Pa? Why have they not come for me?

She wrapped her arms around herself and thought again of home. Of the fireplace and the rocking chair and of Mother—the way her hair smelled when she held her close.

More tears leaked out and she lay on her side, begging for sleep to come.

Click.

She yelped and covered her eyes to the slit of light that suddenly appeared in the room. Her eyes, normally sensitive to light, were beyond painful. She'd been without proper food or light for three days now.

The sound of an old woman's shaky voice. "Sadie, is that you?"

Megan scrambled to her feet. She had no idea what to call this woman. *She?* "Yes, it is me."

"Hurry before they come!" 'she' said.

They joined hands and trotted down the hallway toward the stairs as fast as the old woman could manage.

Footsteps...coming.

'She' pulled Megan into a broom closet, holding her hand over Megan's mouth. They held their breath until the footsteps passed. Leaving the small room, 'she' led her down a spiral staircase to a dirt floored cellar. Huge fires burned here and everything from brooms to empty beds littered the large room.

"You stay here. I will bring you food. If anyone comes, you hide? Do you understand me?"

Megan nodded. She was alone in the dark again, but at least this time she was free.

"How is it that she has escaped again? How has a child let herself out of solitary confinement, when there are only three keys?"

"The key from the nurse's area is missing."

"I see. Search Sonata Messing's room and I believe you will find it."

The alarm sounded so loud, even in the basement, she plugged her ears as tightly as she could. Even muffling the hurt, it cut into her head and was painful. She dropped to her knees, for she knew that sound meant something bad.

Unable to prevent herself, she darted around the cellar without direction or reasoning. Run, get home... the words shouted in her head. Slowing, she paced back and forth on the dirt floor like a caged animal, holding her ears in case of another offensive outburst of noise.

"Sadie, where are you?" The old woman's whispery voice came from the stairs. "Come with me, child."

It was Megan's turn to lead as they exited the door in the kitchen, and onto the grounds. She tried to run and pull 'she' with her, but 'she' was old and moved slowly. They ran across the grounds, keeping to the fence as best they could, 'she' running her hand along it the whole time.

Stopping short, 'she' pulled on Megan's hand. "Here!" 'she' said and pushed on a loose board that moved aside.

Megan slipped through the fence by turning sideways. The thin, frail, old woman was able to fit through the opening, too.

The forest seemed to sigh as the wind whipped through the boughs—twisted tree trunks and bogs surrounded the *Blackhouse*. Cypress trees reminded her of spider webs as she flew past them in the dark. Although scary, the forest was not as frightening as the dark solitary room she'd left behind.

About five minutes after entering the woods, they heard the barking. Dogs! From the sound of them, they were quickly gaining.

"Wolves," said 'she.' "Run!"

The sound of water drew their attention. "There is a river over the hill," 'she' said, pulling Megan in that direction.

Now visible torches bounced up and down through the woods.

The first of the dogs reached Megan, wrapped its teeth around her leg and brought her to the ground. 'She' picked up a tree branch and whacked furiously at the dog's snout as well as her feeble arms could manage. A second bounded into the clearing, its teeth tearing the old woman's flesh like parchment paper.

A third arrived, snarling and snapping at her now prone form on the ground. Feebly 'she' swung her arms to knock it off while blood sprayed from her cut arm.

"Climb the tree, Sadie!"

Megan scrambled to climb, but the dog's jaws bit into her shift, ripping it off. It latched onto her leg and pulled her to the muddy ground.

"Place her into the baths!" she heard a voice bellow from the trees.

~ *Chapter Eleven* ~

Lucian reined the carriage into the circle in front of StoneWater. He jumped down and held up his hand to help Stanzy out. After the toiling end to their Nags Head trip, and the last four days at Hawthorne House with Katrina, she was exhausted.

No matter how often Katrina said she was adjusting to her new post, Constanza had seen she wasn't. Why else seek a way out of her governess role by marrying someone she didn't love? The entire trip back, Stanzy fretted over her sister's lack of good sense and she felt relieved to be back at StoneWater.

"It doesn't seem so long ago that you helped me down out of a carriage when I'd first arrived here. I *knew* then you wanted me."

Lucian's brow lifted. "Is that so? Just how did you *know*?"

"Your hand held mine too long, and you brushed my palm with your thumb."

"Well, come here. I no longer have to keep my thumbs to myself." He reached to pull her to him.

"Miss Constanza! Lucian! Oh, thank heaven ya'll are back. Come inside now. We must talk." Bess' frame was leaning out the downstairs window, her face pinched in distress.

They rushed into the kitchen and sat at the table, looking at her expectantly.

"It is Megan. They took her the night you left. A doctor came and fetched her and carted her off to the asylum."

Never having swooned in her life, Stanzy felt her vision go to a pinprick and the kitchen disappeared as she fought against the spell.

Lucian's arm held her waist tightly. "Constanza. Open your eyes."

She pressed her palms against her forehead. "Where are Ian and Sarah, and where have they taken Megan?"

"He is upstairs in his study. Her royalness has headed back to Bath. They had Megan taken to a place called St. Augustus Lunatic Asylum."

Stanzy and Lucian ran up the stairs and burst into Hopkins' study.

"How could you, Ian?" Lucian accused. "You are a gutless maggot. She is your daughter! I do not care if you get rid of me. This farm will go to the debtors if I go and you know it. You gave in to Sarah, didn't you?"

Ian ran a hand down his face, which looked more lined than ever. "*We* felt it best for Megan."

"We?" queried Stanzy. "Don't you mean Sarah felt it best for her? Do you have any idea what they do to people in asylums, Ian? Well I do! I used to visit them with my father in England, and I will not rest one moment 'til I have Megan back here and out of harm's way! The bleeding is nothing, compared to procedures they may try on her—her with no voice and no way to protect herself against them!"

"Maybe I have been too hasty," Hopkins admitted.

"We are going Ian—now—to get her." She turned to Hopkins. "If you do not want to come, you need to write a letter for us, releasing her into our care."

"Yes, that would probably be best, so I can handle Sarah's wrath when she returns."

After the his governess and Lucian departed from his study, Hopkins retrieved a letter from the desk drawer and read a portion of it once again. He stood and crossed the room to bolt the door.

"Keep Blackwell busy at the ports for whatever reason you can concoct. I have plans that you best not interfere with. Should you choose not to heed my request, I know the lawmen would be very interested in knowing all about your 'special storehouses.' I will be along shortly to discuss this at length..."

As Stanzy lifted herself up beside Lucian on the carriage seat, he said, "What do they do at the asylum?"

She stared straight ahead and said nothing. Some sights were too horrendous to be uttered out loud.

He slapped the reins on the horses to hurry them along.

Megan couldn't stop screaming. After wailing for going on half an hour, a smelly rag was draped over her face. Thrashing against it, her arms soon felt heavy and weak. But she still heard their voices—right up to the point when she surrendered to the peaceful silence inside her mind.

"What is your assessment, Dr. Valleter? Do you think she is possessed?"

"No. The idea is becoming increasingly a superstition in my mind. She is ill, to be sure. The latest treatment plans convey a need for a shock to the system to restore balance. Similar to the blood letting, and you have seen our deep submersion baths I assume?"

"Yes, sir, very impressive."

"We will begin with those and see how she progresses. She may be a candidate for some of our more novel ideas as I believe she is likely to become a resident here, and not for a short-term stay. Reconvene upon the implementation of those treatments so we may plan her next course of treatment."

The river was icy cold, just like she remembered the morning she snuck outside and fell in—Pa had pulled her from the water. It was even colder this morning. At any moment Pa would reach in and pull her out and her body would stop shaking. Her teeth chattered—hard. A wretched taste filled her mouth as she bit her tongue. Slowly opening her eyes a slit, she saw ten pairs of eyes regarding her. Large chunks of ice floated around her in the tub. Her skin burned when the hunks grazed her as they floated past.

No.

The *Blackhouse*—she was still here. She began to cry again, feebly, for she had no strength left. She felt the hoarse sound in her chest when she wailed.

When the darkness crawled into her mind to claim her, she cried out, "Pa, please."

"She spoke," she heard a female voice say. "Get her out of the tank!"

That night, Megan thrashed fitfully on her bed—it was too cold to sleep. She opened her eyes and immediately shut them again as 'the men' were in the room. If they knew she was awake, they may try to do something else to her.

"Dr. Valleter, what is your diagnosis, melancholy or mania?"

"Most decidedly melancholy. How did the treatments progress?"

"It was reported by the staff that while in the baths, she spoke. It is the first time she has uttered a word during any of her admissions."

"Good, she is making progress then. Today, we shall try forced emesis, and see what improvement we attain. Her chart says she was not particularly fond of the bleeding procedure."

Megan rolled over and squeezed her eyes tightly shut as she thought of home, and Ma and Pa, and her soft doll, which she wished she had right now, more than ever. Her breath rattled in and out of her mouth and a deep ache formed in her chest.

Why couldn't she talk? She knew what she wanted to say, could even hear the words in her head, except sometimes they came out wrong, or didn't come out at all when she tried to speak them.

Ma was going to fix her though, she *knew* it. Mother was able to make her feel and think like she never had before.

They would come for her.
They loved her.
They would fight for her.
They would never forget about her.

Unable to help herself, Stanzy continued to cry. The tears poured from her eyes as if they would never cease. *This* was just too much to bear. The thought of what they might be doing to Megan, her wonderful, silent, little girl.

Lucian remained quiet and stared ahead, knowing no words of comfort would calm her. Thankfully, she appreciated that he didn't offer empty platitudes. He was as distraught as she. His knuckles blanched with the force he exerted in holding the reins as the carriage bumped along the windy road. A muscle jutted in his jaw as he gritted his teeth, his lips pressed into a firm straight line.

"We should have just ridden the horses, it would have been faster. This is taking too long!"

"What about when we get her back? You know she won't be able to ride in back of one of us the whole way to StoneWater. The carriage is the only way. Keep your wits. I need you to convince those doctors to release her to us." His hand found hers and squeezed gently.

Calm had settled over his face as she considered him. It quelled her own fears, and she sucked in deep breaths, wrestling to regain her sense of reasoning.

"What if I can't talk them into anything?"

Lucian said nothing, but his hand involuntarily slipped to the pistol strapped to his side.

Constanza shifted in her seat, attempting to alleviate the pain in her bottom. They urged the horses nonstop through the night. Lucian's head bobbed for the third time in an hour and she elbowed his ribs to rouse him.

"Lucian, rest in the back of the carriage for a while. I have the map and can follow where we are going."

"All right. You are going to have to do the same, or your wits will be as dull as mine by the time we arrive at 'The Blackhouse.'" He handed Stanzy the reins and climbed into the rear.

"The Blackhouse?"

"That is what Megan calls it. I never knew what she was talking about until a few weeks ago. When we were outside she was having a particularly good day and said, 'No Blackhouse, Pa.' *This* place was what she meant."

His head dropped to the wagon floor and he closed his eyes.

Stanzy gazed at the gun on his hip and wished fervently for one.

The high-pitched sounds flying from Megan's throat weren't human. Her yowling resembled the eerie scream of baby rabbits, anticipating their death.

"Can't you inject her with something? That voice is splitting my ears. Maybe doctor is correct, she sounds like an animal."

Two men grabbed her arms and two women her feet as they pinned her, spread-out to the bed. Fingers clamped her nose shut. She held her breath as long as she could. Feeling the blackness approaching, she opened her mouth and the rancid taste of the tartar mixture overwhelmed her. She sputtered and gagged, half of the vile drink rising up her throat, the rest bubbling out her nose.

The nasty stuff worked almost immediately. Violently gagging and retching, she dowsed her shift with the remainder of her lunch. Between the gagging and vomiting, the hateful tears came, besetting her chest with painful hiccups. The teardrops spilled over and down her cheeks; she willed her eyes to dry. To end it all, forever—so that this pain called living would stop.

The nurse standing by made eye contact with her. "This is the first time she has ever looked me in the eye."

Megan sat up on the bed, knotting the sheets in her balled fists. She knew her face was twisted and she raged, "I want to go home!"

The staff stood, struck dumb. The four adults gaped at her first with curiosity then amazement. One by one, joining the chorus of sound, they all applauded.

Abernathy followed Teache to the edge of town, to a home the rogue had never visited since he'd had him under observation.

This was disconcerting. Of late, he felt Teache was concocting a plan, the intention of which Abe had been unable to decipher. Each time he felt he had figured out his subject's dealings, the man would add a new person or situation to perplex him. If he didn't know better, he would think Teache was doing it intentionally.

The female who opened the door was of the second set of Teache's women friends. The first set consisted of the unrefined and poor, in whom he would have only specific interests. The second was seemingly well-to-do ladies, whom he had somehow convinced he was a charming merchant seaman.

This woman was beautiful with dark, thick hair piled high atop her head, and her clothing the latest style and trend. Her home, too, was on the good side of town.

Abernathy decided to sit in the pub across the street to wait this one out. He had the feeling it was going to be a long one.

"Stanzy. Wake up."

Nightfall approached as the carriage rattled its way up the lane to the asylum.

Orderlies standing at the entrance eyed them warily as they made their way through the entrance hall. "May we help you?"

"I am here on behalf of StoneWater Estate to collect one Megan Hopkins from your facility to escort her home. Here is the corresponding paperwork." Lucian handed the document to the fellow whose skin was impersonating a ghost, suggesting he hadn't seen daylight in many a fortnight.

"Well, there is nothing we can do for you tonight. The doctors have all retired, so you will have to return in the morning."

"We will not wait another night!" Stanzy spat out, emphasizing each word. Out of the corner of her eye she noticed Lucian's hand stray to rake over his face, but she just could not stop. "Megan will not spend another night here! You tell whatever doctor necessary that he needs to see us now."

"Mum, be reasonable..." But he was cut short by the sound of screaming from a nearby treatment room.

"That is her. I would know her voice anywhere." She darted in the direction of the noise coming down the hallway.

One orderly snatched at her sleeve, thinking her an eloping patient. Stanzy ducked out of his reach and fell to her knees, crawling past him like a scuttling crab. She pushed open the door as soon as she reached it and shuddered at the sight in front of her.

Megan was blue. In a submersion bath filled with bobbing ice cubes. On her tiny arms were the dreaded leeches Stanzy had already removed from her one time this month.

The child's eyes stared vacantly.

"Megan!" she shrieked. "Look at me, poppet!"

"Mama! Please—home—now—no more!" she wailed piteously. Her hands feebly attempted to sign the words she spoke, but plopped into the cold bath.

Lucian pushed into the room just as Constanza stomped over to the bath, plunged her arms in shoulder high and lifted the shaking child from the water.

The staff stood half stunned and gape mouthed. Looks of fear covered their faces.

Clutching Megan's dripping form to her chest, she challenged the stares of each person. "Yes, you better be scared. Your kind will not touch her again. Never again! This is not treatment, this is madness." She strode out the door.

Lucian fell in beside her, matching her stride. She noticed his hand on his holstered pistol, and hoped he wouldn't have to use it.

In the carriage, Constanza pulled Megan's wet clothing from her little form, dressed her in clean clothes Bess had supplied before they left, and wrapped her in a blanket Lucian pulled from the back. She cradled her in her arms as the carriage rattled its way along the road.

The girl hadn't stopped shaking since Constanza had removed her from the submersion tank, but her fingertips were no longer blue. Nor had Megan spoken. Stanzy felt the tears stinging her eyes, but fiercely blinked them away. She must be strong for Megan. She tried to wrap her whole body around the little girl to restore the warmth that horrendous place had sucked from her.

If she and Lucian didn't fight for this little soul, who would? Deep in her heart, she now knew she would never leave StoneWater—not without Megan.

Lucian hadn't spoken since the heated discussion with the doctors about Megan's untimely discharge. She recognized the controlled rage in his posturing, and the set look on his face as he steered the team through the night.

She chanced a glance at him. His posture didn't change, but he placed a hand on her shoulder and gave it a quick squeeze.

Reliability.

An unknown concept to Stanzy. From her earliest memories, she'd learned she could rely on no one but herself. Her mother's care had been loving, but it also had tended to revolve around her father's moods and fits of alcoholic rage.

She tried to block out the recollections, but when she was weak or exhausted, they resurfaced, like unwanted recurring nightmares. Always they scratched behind the door in her head. Subdued, but never forgotten.

Her soul ached for unwavering devotion, and Lucian had given it to her. Someone she could depend on to help shoulder the weight of the world, and he *actually cared* about her thoughts and feelings.

I never thought a man existed who cared for a woman's ideas. Or pain.

Over the years, she'd endeavored to foster in Katrina and Will the sense that they were safe as long as she protected them. She never wanted them to experience the panic she'd felt when she awoke in the mornings— fearful of how their father would act or if she would have to bear the burden of responsibility and intervene in a botched medical procedure.

She looked at Lucian and said a silent prayer of

thanks to God for providing her someone after all of her years of suffering.

"We need to stop at this inn, Constanza. Megan is going to be ill without doubt. It is too cold out here for her, and you are both trembling."

Abernathy sat at the bar, watching Teache out of the corner of his eye.

The evening crowd was rowdy and the noise in the pub had reached new heights. This itinerant life was starting to wear on him. He longed to see his family and sleep in his own bed. The daily assignment of having to watch Teache smuggle, fornicate, and engage in drunken brawls had finally taken its toll. He'd spent so much time in pubs, he wasn't sure if once home, he could ever enter one again.

If he'd been permitted to intervene and not just observe, then perhaps this assignment would have been tolerable.

He longed to have a go at the demon. The man hadn't manifested one redeeming quality to date—not one act of uncharacteristic kindness, no chivalry when no one was looking—nothing to hint there might be a *human* on the inside of this fellow.

Teache seemed exceedingly pleased with himself about something this evening to be sure. That portended nothing good. Abernathy's job was to figure out what that something might be, especially if it pertained to the whereabouts of smuggled items that Governor Spottsswood would consider significant.

What the devil was he doing? Abe Hornigold shifted slightly on the barstool to make himself partially obscured by the patron in front of him. Smoke and whiskey permeated the air of the pub, and with the dim light provided by a few lit candles, Abe thought Teache would be hard-pressed to see him even if he had a mind to.

Teache sat staring intently at a dingy seaman seated across from him. His tattooed fist shook vigorously in front of the man's face. The man shrugged, held out his hand and produced...

Perched on the edge of his seat, Abe was ready for a knife, a pistol, gold...but *a book?*

I must get closer. He picked up his mug and strategically slid behind other patrons until he reached an open table and took a seat, entirely too close to the pirate for comfort. But he needed this assignment to be finished and to do that he needed to see what piece of literature was so compelling that it captured the attention of the infamous pirate.

Teache opened the book with the spine toward Abe, who squinted and peered, cocking his head every which way. Still, he was unable to discern a title.

Again picking up his mug, he walked directly toward Teache. Indeed he had learned typically it was easier to be invisible when you were out in the open for all to see, rather than skulking about.

He passed behind Teache unnoticed and completed his turn at the bar.

His fellow patron on the neighboring stool enquired, "You ill?"

"What? No...why do you ask?"

"You look like you seen a ghost!"

"No, no ghost, just...fairies."

"Well, fairies, then. Ye be careful...they be *more* troublesome than ghosts!"

Abe shook his head, *what in the world could Teache want with a book about fairies?* As he downed his umpteenth glass of ale at the bar, he figured he had suffered enough. He blew into the whistle baked into the mug to get the barkeep's attention.

"Oi, Jim. Let us square up."

It was midmorning when they arrived at the circular path that arched in front of StoneWater leading to the rambling front porch.

"Home," said Megan, the first word she'd spoken since her retrieval from the tank.

When Constanza saw the direction in which Megan was pointing, her heart swelled with an odd combination of pride, anxiety and hope all at once. She was pointing at their cottage, not the manor.

Lucian looked down at her, his brown eyes softening for the first time since last night. "Yes, Meg. Home."

Hopkins was on the porch ready to meet them. Absent was his jaunty step and flashy clothes. Constanza actually felt sorry for him.

He is in the middle with nowhere to go. He has no idea what to do with Megan, but I'm certain he wants the best for her. He is the intermediary between his wicked, self-centered wife and his disabled child.

There was *no* confusion in Constanza's mind as to Sarah Hopkins' wishes. She wished her child had never been born, and her way of coping was to put her out of her sight, preferably miles away, under the guise of expensive housing and treatment, when what Megan really needed was love. Something the rich Hopkinses would never be able to give her.

"Lucian, I need a word in my study. Constanza, take Megan up to her apartment."

And that was it. No hug, no emotion. Megan was property.

After Constanza left with Megan, Lucian readied himself with a huge breath in front of Ian's colossal desk in the study, preparing to receive a browbeating.

Hopkins paced back and forth behind his desk. He started to speak several times, but then would abruptly stop, muttering incoherently.

"Ian, out with it. Just tell me."

"Lucian, I know you care for Megan, and you seem to have been able to draw her out in a way I have not, but I do not know..." He shook his head, then ran his hand over his stubbled face. "If she continues to be...different...I do not know how much longer I can put Sarah off from sending her to, at the very least, a special boarding school."

"I anticipated this day would eventually come. Why don't you give her to me and Constanza to raise? You know in your heart we can do a far better job of it than any boarding school, no matter how special. Give her a chance at a normal life, Ian. We already have helped her to speak."

Hopkins hung his head. "I don't know, Lucian. That is a huge consideration."

"I know it is, and I do not expect an answer today or even next fortnight, but consider it. We want no payment for her either."

"I would not think of burdening you without compensation..."

Lucian narrowed his eyes and peered at Ian across the table. "She is *not* a burden. We want *her*. We do *not* want your money."

"There is another matter." Ian averted his eyes. "There has been an incident...a woman arrived last night asking for you...a very beautiful foreign woman. She is upstairs in one of our guest lodgings. I knew not what else to do with her 'til you arrived."

"What?" Lucian stood to go. When his hand reached for the doorknob, Ian quickly came up behind him and grabbed his elbow to turn him around.

"She is probably seven months pregnant, and she says it is yours."

Lucian's legs wobbled and felt weaker with each step toward facing yet another fiasco. He entered the foyer proper, searching for his supposed impregnated lover. He was a victim of someone's impossible, cruel game, but would Constanza believe him?

He didn't need to ponder it long for Constanza stood at the bottom of the stairwell, quivering as she stared at the dark, exotic woman who, despite being infinitely round, was—at face value—eminently more beautiful than her.

At the sight of him, Stanzy screamed in his face, "You liar!" She launched herself at him, poking him hard in the chest. "I believed *every word* you said to me. I was so stupid. I should have known it could not be real."

"Oh please, I swear, I have never seen this woman before!" Lucian pleaded, his eyes darting frantically to the woman's gargantuan middle. "Constanza, I do not know her and it is not mine!"

"Ow could you say zat, Lucian? After all ve 'ave been thru togedder? You promised you vould take care of me and ze child. I cannot help it if you decided to marry anozer!"

"Leave! Leave now! We do not need you. I will care for Megan and Will and even Ben if you want me to. Just get out of my sight, and take her with you!"

"All right, I will go. If a stranger's word is all it takes to make you doubt my love for you, then maybe our love is not what I thought it was. I will be back for Ben."

The slam of the manor door was so violent, a piece splintered off and fell to the floor.

~ *Chapter Twelve* ~

Abernathy again sat, watching. If he never had to track anything or anyone again, it would be too soon. He feared he would never be able to stomach bird watching, once a favorite activity, as it would feel too much like this despicable situation he found himself in.

I am a voyeur. Brilliant occupation.

Teache sat on his front porch at Hammock House, slitting open the post that had just arrived. His dark face was somber for a moment, then lit up like one of the lighted hemp ropes he so frequently wound into his mangy beard.

His hulking frame stood and he clapped his hands together like a schoolboy and, as if to second the notion, he pulled his pistol and rang off a shot into the air in a sort of odd celebration.

Abernathy's anxiety reached a new level. He was no longer on top of this situation and he knew it.

"Faster, Pilot!"

Constanza squeezed the horse's sides with her legs, urging the stallion on at breakneck speed. He was tired and she knew it, but cared little. His flanks sweated and he galloped slower. Her legs moved in time to his ragged breathing. She kicked him in the sides to pick up the pace. Winding the horse in and out of the stone paths, higher and higher, she drove him on until she reached the summit—where StoneWater was visible in all its glory.

She glared down at the estate as if viewing an amputated limb. Hatred filled her soul, and she spit on the ground—the familiar dead, stony feeling encased her heart. It had tricked her, and nothing had ever tricked her before.

That is what you get for letting your guard down, you stupid woman. He never really loved you. For all you know, he has women like that in every port he does business in.

Full of despair, she wrenched the reins around and drove the horse on again, weaving through dangerously tight paths. Tree limbs smacked her in the face, but she didn't even flinch.

A fallen trunk lay across the path and she urged the mount to vault it. A momentary feeling of weightlessness engulfed her before horse and rider thudded heavily on the other side. The sound of rushing water ahead didn't give her pause or make her halt Pilot. She charged the horse through the stream, feeling the water soak her up to her thighs. On the other side of the bank, the horse slipped and faltered, sliding backward down the slope. His hooves made a sucking sound as he struggled to extract them from the thick mud. She kicked him again, refusing defeat.

"Come on, Pilot!" The horse stutter-stepped and continued his backward descent.

Panicking, the horse's ears laid flat to his head and he reared. Her body catapulted and rolled down the slope, her leg striking a rock. Wet, hot blood poured out as it ripped open a gash. She lay still—afraid to move—afraid to assess the damage. Sitting up, she saw a circle of blood spreading out on her stockings.

Shaking her head, she fought the tears, but they came anyway. She wrapped her arms around her legs and rocked slowly back and forth.

"Oh, Lucian...how could you?"

Somewhere in the back of her mind, a voice whispered...*he couldn't and you know it.*

She dried her tears and sat up straight.

For an irrational moment, fear gripped her, like when she'd been a child in the woods at home. Her mother was full of tales of sprites and goblins, and the woods in which she now sat with her bottom in the mud would be a perfect residence for one of them. Somewhere in the distance a branch cracked, and she thought of her most feared childhood creature, a Spriggan. They mislead weary travelers until they become lost in the woods and then lead them to fall into hidden wells—where they stayed forever.

"All right, enough self-pity."

Whether Lucian *did* or *did not*, she had others to care for. At least three children depended on her—she couldn't be taking risks such as riding at breakneck speeds. It was selfish and irresponsible.

"And goodness knows I can't be selfish even for a minute!" she snarled.

Somewhat painfully, she stood, brushed herself off and went in search of Pilot, who had already crossed the stream, snorting his disgust at her behavior.

"Nags Head. My favorite town on the Banks," the man at the bar slurred, to no one in particular.

Abe watched as the man squinted, evidently trying to focus his vision, the look on his face like one trying to decipher a curious puzzle. The young man attempted merrymaking, but with every guffaw of raucous laughter or bout of singing he seemed to withdraw further into himself. He cradled his mug in his hands tenderly.

Abe blew his whistle in his pint. "Oi! Down ere!"

A young girl tripped past his bar stool, and proceeded down the bar to stumble closer to the young man. Her fingertips traced across his wide shoulder blades as she passed behind him.

"Ooowee, ain't you a strappin' one? Wat's your name love?"

"Lucian." He bestowed a most beguiling smile on the drunken barmaid. He then continued, "Please have mercy, I cannot take another."

Her smile vanished. "No more females?"

Tonight, Abe was heartily enjoying his people watching. Teache was back at Hammock House entertaining, so he had given himself a night off.

The lad down the bar was drunk to be sure, but he'd

been watching him and was exceedingly amused with his wry sayings.

The more the dark-haired man poured into his mouth, the more hilarious the words that leaked out of it. His expression clearly showed he suffered some-thing...so misery loves company.

Abe pulled up a seat at the bar next to him. "Jim, one for me and my new friend here!"

The young man regarded Abe with a critical eye or presumably as close as he could muster in his current condition.

Apparently considering him no threat, he responded blearily. "All right, I'll be your friend if you like. Jus keep 'em comin'!"

They both burst out laughing.

"Lucian Blackwell." He extended his hand to Abe in greeting.

And throwing caution to the wind, he gave the man next to him his real name for the first time in more than a year. "Abernathy Hornigold. Abe for short."

"All right, Abe. What brings you to Nags Head?"

"Umm...I am on an assignment."

"I see." The young man stared him in the eye, momentarily becoming serious. "Is it a secret?"

"Why, yes, it is."

Lucian's mouth twitched. "Mine, too. But I will tell ye, ya seem like a nice enough sort. I am here to forget my troubles, and to complete the mission—become as drunk as humanly possible."

"So I observed! What seems to be the problem?"

And so began a tale which Abe took as uncharacter-istic flippancy for the young man sitting at his side—a sordid story beginning with Lucian's hands reaching into the surf to retrieve a young woman, to slamming the door and leaving her, and now ending up in this bar.

The bartender made his last call as Lucian finished his story, and as Hornigold had stopped drinking at about the third mention of Teache's name, he was beginning to feel quite sober.

"Well, Lucian, you seem like an upstanding fellow,

but putting it plainly, you have made a very serious enemy in Edward Teache. If he has set his sights on your wife, and he is a man not accustomed to being turned down no matter the situation, I am afraid her safety may still be in question."

Lucian blinked and shook his head fiercely. "Even though we are married, you think he is still going to pursue her?"

"Oh, that means nothing to Teache. Any woman or object is game to him, regardless of their station in life. Well, let us reason this out. If what you say is true, and you are innocent of an infidelity, where do you think that woman came from?"

A look of amazement dawned on Lucian's drunken face. "No! If he did that, he will stop at nothing to get...and I left her and the children alone! I am so stupid!" he said, smacking his head to second the notion.

He'd stumbled off his stool and reached for his overcoat when Abernathy reached for his arm. "Whoa, there, young fella! You are in no condition to head anywhere tonight. Where are your lodgings?"

Lucian gestured a finger to the ceiling.

"Then let's get you to your room upstairs and I promise at first light, I will wake you and follow you to StoneWater. I want to ask your wife some questions, if it is all right with you."

"You were not jesting about your station, were you?" Lucian said darkly.

Abernathy didn't reply. He remained silent the whole way up the stairs to the sleeping rooms.

"I am across the hall, in case of any disturbances. Just give a holler."

Sometime later, Abernathy was just entering a dream—a wonderful dream about his home when he heard shuffling and a commotion outside his door.

Opening it a crack, Abe peered out into the hallway. A lady of the evening appeared to be attempting entry into Lucian's room.

Lucian was closing the door as gently as possible,

saying, "Please, ma'am, there is some misunderstanding, I made no inquiry as to a visitor to my room."

As soon as Abernathy sensed the danger, it was too late. A pistol flashed out from under the woman's shift and she pointed it at Lucian's chest. Abe sprang across the hall, but Lucian managed to redirect the shot from his heart to his arm. Lucian was shirtless and Abernathy watched in horror as blood spurted from the gunshot wound.

Abernathy restrained the woman. "Help! Someone call a doctor!"

Lucian had been gone only a few days, but it seemed like an eternity to Stanzy. It was amazing how she hadn't realized the extent to which he had colored her life. A note lay open on the cottage table. She'd just returned from checking on another of the ill slaves, when she sat to read it.

It was in Sarah Hopkins' hand:

"Constanza.

"Your presence is formally requested tonight at the Manor to dine at five in the evening. We are expecting guests and Ian insists that you attend. Wear your best.

"Mrs. Hopkins"

The absolute last thing I wish to do is feign politeness and sit in a room with a bunch of tittering women who wouldn't know substance if it introduced itself to them.

Knowing that refusal was useless, she relented to the task of making herself presentable.

As she walked slowly toward the main house, she felt like she was being led to slaughter instead of a party. On approaching the porch, she noticed one of the men arch an eyebrow when he saw her. Looking down at her dress, she flattened it self-consciously. Did men actually find her attractive?

Maybe I will wave to him with my left hand, and watch his expression change.

The party consisted of three women and three men, all of whom were equally vapid. Their names escaped her, though they had been introduced only moments before. Her brain was fixated on Lucian.

All sat to dine, and her face flushed so violently she thought she might faint when none other than Edward Teache slid into the empty chair next to her. Everyone in the room greeted him as if he were a long, lost brother. Her stomach churned to see every female eyelash in the room bat at him.

He, however, didn't take his eyes from her. "Allo, Constanza! How are you? I bring greetings from Bath."

After his hand *accidentally* brushed hers for the fifth time, it became apparent he was trying to touch her in any way possible, and it made her skin crawl. It became increasingly difficult with each passing second not to scream and run from the table. She quit speaking after about five minutes, not trusting what might burst forth from her mouth.

After dinner the men retired to the drawing room for brandy, and the ladies for tea in the sitting room.

Stanzy excused herself. In the hallway she leaned against the wall, willing it to hold her up. She cracked open the front door and deeply breathed in fresh air.

"I think the salt air would be preferable to the smell of manure," said a deep voice from down the hall.

The shadows hid his face, but she knew it was him. It was glaringly obvious he'd been waiting for her to leave the company of the women to confront her.

He ambled up beside her, cockily propping his arm against the wall and peering down into her face. "I have something for you."

For one wild moment, when he reached into his coat pocket, she was certain it would be a pistol. But no—he extracted a tiny silver box and opened it for her to see what was inside.

Stanzy had never seen a piece so beautiful. The ring was encrusted with every jewel she'd ever seen and some she hadn't. Plucking it from the box, he held it up to the light, the flickering candlelight making colored prisms dance around the entryway.

"I wanted to be sure that you had not changed your

mind, and wanted to ask you to reconsider being my bride."

What a clod! She wanted to scream at him and pummel that bloody barrel chest with her fists—but he was huge and could snap her like a hollow reed, if so inclined.

"I thought your heart belonged to my sister, Katrina? She has told me that you have asked for her hand."

He looked straight in her eyes. "She is just a substitute for you, Constanza. But you know that already, don't you? Never met a woman as shrewd as you before."

She dropped her eyes, her brain frantically weighing all of her options. "You know I am already married." She held up her ring for him to see, its tiny stone glimmered faintly.

"To a man who would so easily cast you aside for another woman? Like a common whore?"

"How dare you! You do not fool me. You may fool my sister, because she is young and was born foolish, but I see you for what you really are. And even if my husband did lay with another woman, he is still a greater man than you could ever hope to be!"

Half expecting to feel a lead ball in her back, she turned and, head held high, strode straight out the front door. When it didn't come she bolted full force toward her cottage.

Stanzy sat at the hearth in the cottage by the fire. Unable to sleep, she held the musket on her lap.

Ben and Will were in bed, sound asleep. After she was sure all of the guests had departed from the manor, she'd checked on Megan. Satisfied she was all right, she'd returned to the cottage. Megan hadn't protested being taken to the manor instead of the cottage—probably anywhere was better than the asylum.

Comforted everyone was in bed safe, yet tonight it felt tainted, like the taste of cider in your mouth right before it turns rancid. She shot up and paced back and forth. At this rate she would wear a hole in the floor by year's end. She felt if she had to stay in the house tonight she would go mad. Hastily, she scribbled a note so, if the boys awoke, they would know where she'd gone. She propped it against the bowl sitting in the middle of the table.

Angry at herself was an understatement. Never had she permitted someone to see inside her mind, making her thoughts vulnerable, *even admitting she could be vulnerable.*

Pilot protested at being taken out in the dark, but she saddled him anyway. She rode him through the fields, where Lucian toiled every day with the slaves he considered and treated as brothers.

She rode past the manor to the stone wall surrounding all the acres, and began to trace her way along it. She had to sort out her feelings.

Do I still love him?

Unfortunately, yes.

She thought of Aunt Rose, and the way she spoke of him. A forthright woman, very much like herself. Reflectively, she considered what she would say to a woman if Stanzy knew Will were being unfaithful. No question in her mind, without hesitation she would tell the woman and give Will a *what for*. Stanzy would let him know in no uncertain terms she'd raised him better than that.

For the better part of an hour she rode, coming to the conclusion that Rose most likely would have done the same for her. Now she'd misjudged him, possibly undermining their relationship in her lack of ability to trust him.

When she saw the sun rising in the east, she knew her responsibilities would not wait. Self-indulgently permitting herself a dream, Stanzy wondered what it would be like to refuse to take the correct and proper course, and just return home and stay in bed all day.

As she came up the lane to home, the mail rider approached. One letter was addressed to her. She ripped open the envelope so quickly, she tore part of the letter off in her haste.

"Dear Mrs. Blackwell,

"I am writing on behalf of your husband, Lucian, whom I have had the pleasure of making the acquaintance of in Nags Head. There has been an accident and your presence is requested..."

Stanzy couldn't believe it. She checked out the covered coach window again, trying to assess how much farther it was to Nags Head. Her stomach reeled with anxiety and on several occasions, she had to talk herself through not forcibly removing one of the team horses and riding it bareback to speed up the trip.

During the night she'd obsessed over the whole situation—cried, gotten angry, cried again. Now, she was just plain anxious. How could she have thought Lucian would do such a thing? He was the most openly honest man she'd ever encountered. The more she thought of it, Lucian would have admitted committing adultery before trying to deceive her.

The coach pulled up at the SeaWard Inn, and she practically bolted from the carriage, not waiting for the driver to help her out.

Why start being conventional now?

"Just leave my bags in the lobby!" she yelled over her shoulder to him. She could barely breathe as she bounded to the top of the stairs. A gentleman she guessed to be in his late forties stood waiting for her.

"Constanza Smythe?"

"Blackwell, sir."

"Well, it is a good sign you are still acknowledging you've taken my last name..." issued a voice from behind a partially closed door.

"Lucian?" She tore into the room and flung herself about his neck, where he lay supine on a cot.

"Are you all right?" Immediately she started to unwind the bandages covering his gunshot wound.

"They just dressed it!" He grabbed her face with his hand and kissed her hard.

She broke his hold to regard him, her eyes glistening, and she realized his were too. Each acted as stubborn as the other and refused to speak first.

She capitulated, her voice barely a whisper. "It wasn't yours, was it?"

He met her eyes and shook his head.

"I think I always knew that."

~ *Chapter Thirteen* ~

The sun was just a sliver in the east as Stanzy made her way across the plantation. She pulled her wrap tighter, the weather having turned colder by the day. Oh, it would be wonderful to experience a few days of peace, but she was sure that wouldn't happen anytime soon. It seemed she was only permitted precious few weeks out of the year where she could be happy. Since Lucian's near death experience with the whore, she awoke each morning with unbidden anxiety.

Although you would never know anything happened to look at Lucian. He is all kindness and joy. Unlike me.

Lucian's arm was healing well, and he often refused her attempts to tend to it, reiterating, "It's fine, leave it."

Bess waited for her on the porch of the slave quarters and shuffled her inside, shutting the door behind them.

"Who is ill, Bess?"

"It is Stephen, the fool. I am not gonna lie to you, Miss Constanza. That boy is always getting into the hidden storehouses of rum at the main house. He is drunk as a skunk, as well as ill. He is over there on the cot by the fire."

Stanzy hurried over, knelt beside the cot and proceeded to examine him. She gagged from the strong stench of rum. His hands shook involuntarily and drool seeped from the side of his mouth in a thick, white foam.

"Stephen. Stephen, answer me. Look at me."

The young slave made no indication he'd heard her speak. His eyes slit briefly, revealing the whites before rolling back into his skull once again. His body shook more violently, setting the cot to banging off the floor.

"Does he drink often?"

"Yes, he does. Most every day he can be seen sneakin' somethin' or other."

"It is probably alcohol palsy. We saw it frequently in Bristol."

"What?"

"It is a drinking disease, Bess."

She proceeded to tell Bess the ingredients she would need for the herbal concoction she'd prepared so many times in the past—cayenne, chili powder, cinnamon and sugar. Relating to Bess how to prepare it, she then told her to have Stephen drink it daily and, of course, stay away from the rum.

Sadly, she remembered the first time her mother had taught her how to brew it for her father—she'd been only seven years old. A mere whiff of it brought to mind her father's face...and fist.

As Constanza left the quarters, she noted the roof. Moss grew everywhere, except running down the center was a peculiar sight—a stark line with no moss. As if God's finger had drawn an Almighty singular stroke. She made a mental note to consult her walking, talking seasonal almanac as to what could cause such a phenomenon.

Abernathy Hornigold's wits were trying to pour out his ears. His strict puritan upbringing to control his emotions wrestled with his righteous indignation as he slowly unraveled the life of one Edward Teache.

A man of principle himself, a family man with six children and one devoted wife, the more this plot unwound before him, the more his hatred for Teache grew exponentially.

He knew to expose himself now would likely find him a court-marshal and no effective way to support his substantial brood of children, but emotions he usually held tightly in check were boiling at the top of his searing mind. After seeing the Blackwells off, he'd returned to his post.

He lagged behind as the carriage he followed lumbered its way around the bend, stopping in a wooded area with a winding brook in view.

"Oh no, the scalawag. Does he mean to merely rape the governess or kill her, too?" he asked himself, aware that he'd been acting alone and clandestinely far too long. "Why she cannot be as old as my eldest daughter. I shall not stand by and watch this."

He observed Teache and the young woman amble down the path into the woods, talking quietly—too quietly for him to hear—and laughing. Keeping out of sight, he followed them for a quarter of a mile, losing sight of them in an attempt to remain undetected.

"Blast! Where did you go?"

Then he saw them, on a blanket by the clearing, and, by the looks of the situation, about one breath's moment from a loss of chastity. He dug his heels into his horse and slammed down the trail, intentionally breaking every branch in his wake.

Mission accomplished.

He watched Teache scramble off fair lady, and the look of horror on her young face was perfect—hopefully perfect enough to bring her to her senses!

"Good day, sir! I hope I did not disturb you and your wife? I thought I heard a gunshot from this area and I was just investigating its source."

Teache all but glowed with fury. He stood up to his full height and glared at Hornigold, certain if fair lady wasn't sitting nearby, he would already be dead. Indeed, he may still be dead despite her presence.

"I heard no such shot. I suggest you be on your way, sir. And let my wife and me enjoy our day together."

Hornigold urged the horse forward, fully realizing he may have compromised his mission. But as he watched the girl gather up the blanket and her skirts, then walk back up the trail, he knew it had been worth it.

He'd stopped the naive from sleeping with the devil himself.

The puppy squirmed fitfully, trying to break her hold on it, and Constanza worried it was going to kill itself if she dropped it down the stairs.

"Stop it. Hold still," she chastised, attempting to kick open the door to Megan's apartment. The child lay in her bed, the covers over her head, as she'd been from the previous day. No words had been spoken for many days by their beautiful little one, but Constanza was bound and determined to pull them out of her today.

Stanzy sat on the end of the bed and bounced up and down on it wordlessly.

Megan peeked out from beneath the covers and squinted at her.

Encouraged, Constanza scrambled upright on the bed and jumped gleefully up and down, laughing as she did so. Finally, despite herself, Megan started to laugh. Then she, too, stood on the bed and jumped alongside Stanzy.

"There is my girl!"

Constanza then brought the puppy from the other room and sat him on Megan's lap. Megan stroked the dog in hard even strokes and—eyes shifting to Stanzy then back at the puppy—began to laugh again.

"Dog," Stanzy said and simultaneously performed the sign.

"Dog." Meg parroted.

"Wahoo!" Constanza whooped as she twirled around in circles, reminding herself of a game she used to play as a child where she would spin until she could spin no more. She refused to believe the girl possessed any malice as she watched her stroke the new pup.

Edward Teache rode his horse hard. Sweat streamed off her flanks despite the cold weather. Once he reached town, he dismounted in front of the saloon, pushing his way through the dark smoky crowd to the bar. He was no fool and knew the near mishap the other day with Miss Katrina had been no accident. A careless fool followed him, but he had no idea who, or why. And he was good and tired of that farmer as well. He'd tried to be discreet, but when that failed...well...it wouldn't be the last time he'd had to take what he wanted by force.

Whoever was following him, though, could be certain that if they met in an alley, it would be the end for him. It had nearly cost him his betrothal to Katrina. She was his favorite betrothed so far, second only to her sister.

"Stanzy, I am not going. I will tell Hopkins this is not an appropriate time for me to be traveling to port." Lucian chewed his lower lip and gazed out the window into the fields.

She noticed the early morning light betrayed the slight trace of crow's feet forming around her beloved's eyes.

"Too much has transpired," he added.

"You worry too much," she replied. "Do not be vexed. The boys and I will be fine."

"I cannot put my finger on it. I just do not feel right leaving you. It is as if 'round every corner trouble is waiting to pounce on us."

She slipped up behind him and laid her head against his back. "True, we have endured many unforeseen circumstances, but surely Providence will permit us space to breathe. You will not be tempted beyond what you can bear," she teased.

She felt the broad strength in his back relax. "Ah. Well, I am sure someone as headstrong and utterly impossible as you can mind herself and the lads. I acquiesce. I will be back in a month. If anything untoward happens, send post to the port and I will be back as fast—"

In one quick movement, she placed a finger to his lips to silence him, then wrapped her arms around him. Momentarily, all else in the world faded away.

"Pa, when will you be back?" Ben and Will burst through the door, returning from the barn.

"Manners, boys," Lucian scolded halfheartedly. "Soon. You watch over your mom and the farm. I am counting on you. You know where all the muskets are kept?"

"Yes, Pa."

Lucian quickly left the kitchen after ruffling the hair on the boys' heads.

Later, Stanzy sat on the back porch and stared out into the woods. The uneasy feeling had tripled since Lucian departed for the ports to conduct his business exchanges. Recently she felt the line between reality and her memories of childhood was beginning to blur.

From infancy she'd believed all the tales of the magical creatures her mother remembered from her Irish descent, passed on from generation to generation. Then the days of her father had begun, making her mindset change drastically to one of extreme realism.

Her father had been fiercely pragmatic, so much so that it had drowned out every bit of creativity Stanzy had inherited from her mother. She'd forgotten all about fairies, except for the precious few times she'd told Kitty and Will some of their mother's stories when they were tiny.

With the history of mental illness in her family, and the recent jaunts of her mind to her troubled past, she was seriously beginning to question her sanity. First, the appearance of the Dollahan in the fields, and then the possible changeling she'd delivered. It was as if her Irish past were invading her mind and insisting she acknowledge it.

The forest captured her attention as she spied an odd multitude of fireflies. Exquisitely lighting up the cypress trees, the beetles danced in a choreographed pattern that resembled a smattering of stars across a darkened sky. The sheer number of them made it impossible to look away.

She sucked in breath through her teeth, then froze. A flame streaked through the swarm of fireflies, whisking through their gathering like a comet. Jack, sitting beside her on the porch, rumbled low in his chest; his hackles rising in warning at the sight of the flame.

"Sit, Jack!"

He barked his displeasure and took off for the brush toward the suspended fire.

She charged after him. An ominous feeling rose in her chest, intuition screamed this might not be a wise choice.

Jack had entered the mouth of the woods and had been swallowed whole.

"Jack!" She pelted headlong into the trees, searching wildly for him. The dog was nowhere to be found, and neither was the source of the mysterious fire.

As quietly as possible, she picked her way through the underbrush, all the while scanning and listening with her whole body for any signs of Jack.

Where are you? Why does everything have to happen the moment Lucian leaves StoneWater's lands?

Movement flashed at the corner of her eye, and she whipped her head around in time to see a whisk of flame disappear over an embankment. She picked up her pace, heading in the direction where she'd seen the light. The air developed a surreal quality, and she was surrounded. The fireflies swarmed into the woods. Thousands of them flickered on and off, forming a lighted net all around her. When she tried to walk toward the direction of the flame, they would swarm and impede her progress.

As if struck dumb, she stood wondering if she'd indeed stepped into one of the enchanted forests from her childhood readings.

Finally, she relented and turning on her heel, headed in the opposite direction. The swarm broke apart with her decision. Hurrying down the alternate path, it parted, permitting her to quicken her pace.

Jack lay sprawled on the ground, his foot wedged between two abnormally large tree roots. By its grossly twisted angle, she knew his foot was broken.

Snap.

The breaking branch sounded so close the hairs on her neck rose in alarm. Someone, or something, was in the woods. Watching them.

Snap, snap, snap.

Footsteps echoed in the forest, crashing through the brush without any attempt at surprise.

Pulling at Jack's foot, she tried to dislodge it from the woody trap. He let out a great yelp and struggled to stand, making it more difficult for her to free him.

"Stop it, Jack!" She pulled again at his paw, aware the snapping drew nearer. The underbrush was breaking faster.

"Release *him!*" she yelled at the root. Yanking with all her strength, the twisted brambles parted to free his foot. In disbelief, she shook her head and hoisted the Sheep dog over her shoulders, dashing for the forest exit.

Leaping over a log, her toes tangled in its branches and she plummeted to the ground.

The sound, *snap, snap,* drew ever nearer.

"Will!" Stanzy screamed in desperation from her position on the ground. She struggled to stand with the dog atop her shoulders.

Will's voice then penetrated her conscience.

"Stanzy, where are you?" His voice trembled in fright.

"Will! Get the musket!"

Legs burning as she ran pell-mell for the opening in the trees, she forced herself to keep running, despite the weight of the dog. A blow to her head caused her to lose her footing again, and although careening forward, she managed to stay on her feet. A low undercurrent of sound arrived, and out of nowhere a hailstorm struck with gale force winds.

Breaking free from the forest into the grassy clearing, *its* ragged breathing came in spurts close behind her. She ran on, not chancing a glance; sure that a glimpse of its face would push her to madness.

A shot rang out. Will stood on the porch, aiming toward the woods to her left.

"Run!" he yelled as he let another charge fly.

At last reaching the porch, she collapsed, laying the dog at Will's feet. She whipped around to see the creature, but the only thing she saw were the fireflies once again.

"Did you see what it was?" she asked Will anxiously.

"No. But its shadow had almost overtaken you when you reached the grass." He put his arms around her, and unsteadily said, "Stanzy?"

Following his gaze she stared into the sky. There was no hail to be seen anywhere, but there were frogs.

Everywhere.

They hopped through the hail that had previously fallen in the cottage yard, and littered the steps. The rain barrel overflowed with their slimy bodies that tumbled out in macabre freefalls from all its sides.

Croaking filled the air surrounding the cabin and she hugged Will tightly to her, wishing she'd *never* read a fairie tale in her life.

The days crawled by. Stanzy sat in her rocker by the fire.

Ridiculous. He is just a man. You are fine without him. Stop dwelling on him—on his smell and on his broad back. Stop it! He will be home soon.

Never had she permitted someone to know her so fully—for herself. Except Will of course. She pushed away the thoughts of a colorless life with Lucian. His fiasco with the foreign beauty gave her a glimpse of what life could return to, and the feelings left in its wake were cold and terribly lonely. An ache that started in her womb and spread to her chest engulfed her. She longed for a child with him, so that part of them would always be together.

She hoisted herself from the rocker, took a deep breath, and rallied to the task of teaching Megan. She grinned at the thought of her. Over the past two weeks she'd been able to take her out of her room several times, all without incident. First, she took her horseback riding, which Megan loved, and elicited so much language that Stanzy began keeping a medical record of her advancements. Twice she accompanied Stanzy to sup at the servants' kitchen table—without her parents' knowledge of course—and actually requested simple items she desired without tantrums or violence. Her signs were so fast and furious Stanzy often had trouble keeping up with the conversation.

Stanzy walked through the courtyard, the cold November wind cutting through her shawl. Fear bit at her gut with the thought of Meg's fate if she ever left the governess position at StoneWater. Someday Lucian might want to leave for another county, that is if he ever decided to come back home to her. But she didn't think she could bear to leave Meg, nor she knew, could Lucian. Megan was the primary reason Lucian had remained at StoneWater. That and the fact he was owed thirty acres bequeathed to him by the late, great Mr. Kirkaldy. Mrs. Hopkins' father, Theodore Kirkaldy, had cherished Lucian from boyhood, even over his two daughters, whom he had regarded as silly and insensible creatures.

Opening the servants' entrance door she halted dead in her tracks. Sarah Hopkins stood waiting for her in the kitchen, tapping her scrawny leg impatiently. Stanzy had only seen the mistress in the kitchen once since her arrival.

Bess stood behind her, a look on her face which said, 'Hold ya tongue.'

The woman didn't hesitate. "Constanza. It has come to my attention that my daughter has tolerated going out of doors daily for the past several weeks without incident. I am very pleased with your progress. Therefore, I would like you to have her ready for tea today, by one o'clock this afternoon, in the drawing room. Several important ladies are visiting, and I would like nothing better than for them to see my beautiful daughter."

"Umm, it is true, mum, that she has tolerated being outside, but I really do not feel she is ready for any sort of—"

"*Your* feelings are of no consequence here. She is my daughter and you will do as I say. One o'clock sharp," she snapped, turned, and with her nose in the air vacated the kitchen.

Stanzy hurried up the steps to Meg's apartment, Bess following at her heels. "Her royal tusspot has gone and bit off more than she can chew this time."

Abernathy sat in his room above the inn and examined his notes. This assignment was slowly driving him to pull out what little hair he had left. The wretched perfunctory spying on such a villain was taking its toll on his countenance.

"10 Novembre 1718

"To Governor Alexander Spottswood, Virginia

"Born Edward Drummond—or, possibly, Edward Teache, from Bristol, England—his direct ancestry, I have been unable to discover as yet. He had begun his marauding career on a Jamaican sloop in 1713 as a crewman, under the pirate Benjamin Hornigold, a coincidence that I have extreme distaste for, and then by the spring of this year of our Lord 1718, Blackbeard, as I have begun to refer to him, had in his command four vessels, and up to 300 crewmen, until this May. His ships, *Queen Anne's Revenge* and the *Adventure*, were lost at Beaufort Inlet, not far from where I am writing this journal. I have been made aware that Stede Bonnet 'the gentleman pirate' as he is called (as if there were such a creature!), who once sailed with Blackbeard, escaped the fate of his crewmen, who were all hanged two days previous to this one. He is said to be at large and in hiding. I thought you should know that Blackbeard double-crossed Bonnet in May when the ships were marooned, so he will probably not provide any information as to the whereabouts of Bonnet.

"As per our discussions, you were right in surmising that Teache is continuing his marauding ways, even after the pardon from Governor Eden. I believe, Governor Spottswood, that you should indeed send the Royal Navy to intervene in his treachery. Rumrunning, piracy, and murder, possibly rape, just to name a few of his current infringements on the pardon as he continues to wreak havoc on the locals, who are just now recognizing him for what he is."

Abe stood and stretched his lanky frame. He gazed out at the harbor and knew he could be idle no longer. Teache was forever up to no good. It was imperative he find him again as soon as possible and intervene.

~ *Chapter Fourteen* ~

Constanza forced down Megan's hands from her frilly frock for the twentieth time.

"Listen to me, sweet pea. Your mama wants you to wear this dress. I know it feels itchy, just leave it on a while and then we will come back upstairs and put your shift on."

Meg pulled at her collar. "You are Mama. Not that... other lady."

"No honey, she is Mama."

Megan shook her little head in disagreement, tossing curls back and forth, but said nothing further.

As Stanzy led Meg by the hand down the front grand staircase, the child's legs shook so badly she lost her footing. Halting Megan at the bottom, she straightened the girl's dress one last time.

In the drawing room sat four of the best-dressed females Stanzy had ever laid eyes on. Each smiled sweetly at Megan, who indeed looked absolutely beautiful with her black curls all combed out and lying on her back—try as she might, Stanzy still couldn't get the little thing to tolerate anything in her hair, due to her oversensitive skin and hair follicles.

Stanzy led Megan into the room, placed her on a stool and sat directly behind her on a chair, poised to intervene at the slightest outburst from her pupil.

Katrina took her finger and gently traced it along the line of the mantel. Mrs. Drummond's house was immaculate and beautiful, and she was married to a sailor. Katrina was filled with envy. What an exciting life she must lead with her husband bringing home gifts to her from all over the world, and the waiting for him after months of not being together. Indeed, if Edward Teache were to ask for her hand, she would accept his proposal. So what if he was overzealous to bed her. What man would not be? She smiled at her reflection in the looking glass above the mantel, giving her hair a little flip.

Her reverie stopped short when her eyes fixed across the room and landed on a portrait.

She headed in that direction straightaway, so single-mindedly she almost tripped on her petticoats. Then her mouth dropped and her insides squirmed. Katrina felt violently ill at the sight before her.

The portrait of Mr. and Mrs. Drummond was indeed beautiful. The only problem was the man in the picture was supposed to be *her* betrothed.

It was Edward. Edward Teache!

She plopped hard in the chair behind her, and the room threatened to go black. But she willed it back with her anger, intently staring at the portrait.

Her mind raced through the previous months at the townhall dances, and the words echoed in her head: *"They are never all into port at the same time, so we have never met one another's husbands."* And the tide of massive pregnant bellies swam into view as well. That was when she actually retched.

Her hands flew to her middle again, and she inadvertently spoke out loud. "He almost had me, too, my chastity—and me...*so willing* to give it to him."

Angry tears spilled and she furiously swiped them away with the back of her hand.

Mrs. Drummond hurried her descent down the stairs, as fast as her stomach would allow, at the sight of Katrina's tears.

"Katrina darling, whatever in the world is wrong?"

"Elisa, we have to talk." *And I have quite a few homesteads to visit*, she added under her breath...

Bess entered the sitting room and handed Meg a cup of water, as she refused to drink tea.

"So far, so good..." was all she'd muttered when all

order disintegrated.

Megan flung her head backward and tumbled off the stool to the floor, her shrill shrieks echoing through the manor. The ladies covered their ears in fright, and stared first at her, and then her mother with revulsion. Megan's limbs shook and her head banged off the wood floor as the fit ravaged her body.

Stanzy dropped to her knees. "Bess! Help me!"

Bess flew back into the room and knelt at Megan's feet. They tried to keep her from hitting any nearby objects as her tiny frame violently quivered.

"What is wrong with her?" said her mother, from across the room.

"I will tell you what is wrong with her. The Hopkinses are being punished for their sins, they both love their belongings entirely too much!" said the most elegantly dressed lady.

Stanzy barely heard the woman's words. All she could think of was how she was going to save this child from an awful fate. She looked to the floor and her eyebrows knit together; the dregs of water at the bottom of Megan's cup contained water tainted yellow.

Katrina swatted the reins on the chestnut's flanks. She wanted the horse racing at least as fast as her mind.

How was this possible? Could Edward really have fathered all these children? She thought of his forceful advances and her mind screamed, *Yes!* How many children had been at the town dances she'd attended, twelve? Fifteen?

Fifteen pairs of small brown eyes from the town dance filled her memory. Eyes the color of chocolate— like their father's.

As she stepped through the gate of the white picket fence, Mrs. Thatcher stood hanging sheets on the line to dry. Around her in the yard were her three-year-old twin boys, fighting over a kite. Her six-year-old girl handed her pieces of wash from the overflowing basket at her feet. The woman's rotund middle made it impossible to bend and retrieve them herself. Through her thin shift, her protruding belly button was clearly visible.

Katrina swallowed hard. How was she going to shatter this woman's life?

"Good day, Katrina!" said Alissia as she waved her chubby arm in greeting. This woman was perpetually happy. Katrina had fleeting thoughts that perhaps she should leave it alone. Once these words were spoken, the lives of this woman and her children would be forever altered.

"Hello, Alissia. It is good to see you."

"Come. Let's have some tea, deary, and tell me what brings you here?"

Inside, Katrina sat at the table and Alissia handed her a cup. The boys raced around the table smacking one another. Thankfully, their mother called a halt to their warfare. "Enough! Take it outside!"

Alissia's expression turned shrewd. Staring at Katrina, her eyes narrowed. "What is going on Katrina? You look...well...forlorn. I have never seen you wear it, and it does not become you!"

"How many years have you been married?"

"Why? For six and one-half years, why do you ask?"

"I really do not know how to say this, so please just take a look at this."

She reached into her bag and retrieved the portrait she'd taken from Mrs. Drummond's house.

Alissia's eyes widened and before Katrina knew what was happening, the huge woman slid off the chair, collapsing onto the floor in a heap.

An hour later, Katrina handed her a handkerchief as Alissia repeatedly dabbed her eyes.

"How many are there?" Alissia said pointedly.

When Katrina didn't answer, the distraught woman's voice raised to a shriek. "How *many*?"

"Truly, I am not certain, but I am set on finding them all and telling them."

Horse's hooves clopped up the stoned lane. Katrina shot to standing so quickly she sent the kitchen chair clattering to the floor as she raced to the window.

"It's bloody Edward! I have to get out of here, and my carriage is out front."

"Go! Hurry. I will walk down to the lane and try to distract him. Take the southern exit."

Katrina's heart was beating so hard she felt as if she might pass out. Her breath flew in and out in furious spurts, but she couldn't catch it. She wondered how many of the women she would be able to reach, as Edward was certain to figure out her plan. She dashed as fast as her legs would take her down the southern path. She was determined to reveal his ruse to as many of his wives as she could before fleeing to StoneWater.

Stanzy had been right about him—and oooohhh! She *hated* it when her sister was right.

A carriage approached, its rumble not far off, so she vaulted to the side of the road into the thicket. She peered through the brambles at the passing carriage, her breath whistling out in relief. It wasn't Teache. She waited until the carriage turned at the bend in the road and continued on. Recognizing it at once, she made her way up the lane to the Threacher's home.

She knocked on the door; the afternoon air seemed too still and silent.

Mrs. Threacher opened the door, her eyes were red and bloodshot to match her flaming red hair, which stood out at all angles. "Aloo, Katrina."

"Yes, allo, Katrina," said the voice of evil from behind her.

Katrina turned and bolted from the porch, heading toward the barn. She flung open the door and unharnessed the only horse already saddled and kicked him hard as she headed for the woods.

She glanced back toward the farm and spied Teache's carriage hidden behind the barn.

She could hear the horse's snorts on the trail behind her. She should have ridden her horse down the road. If he caught her on this trail, no one would hear her screams.

The sound of hooves drew closer as she urged the horse into an open clearing. She kicked his sides like mad, but it appeared Teache had chosen the younger horse. She could almost hear him breathing. His horse pulled parallel to hers, and Teache leaped across onto her horse, knocking her sideways from the saddle to the ground.

Before she lost consciousness, she heard him snarl, "That will be enough of talking to my wives. You could be my favorite, Katrina. As a matter of fact, *you will* be my favorite."

From her prone position on the ground, she felt a ring slip onto the fourth finger of her left hand.

Constanza heard them coming before she saw them. She automatically stood and grabbed the musket from beside her and dead bolted the door.

Bang! Bang! Bang!

"Who's there?"

"Mrs. Blackwell, it's me Alphonse. Come quick! Something right terrible is going on!"

Abernathy shifted in the saddle again, his sores had sores, and he adjusted his spyglass to try and locate the devil again. Teache was somewhere ahead of him on the road beneath, returning to Hyde County from Beaufort. Abe had a bad feeling about this. Teache had hurriedly left Hammock House after his attempt to soil the young girl's virginity had been interrupted. As far as Abe had been able to track, Teache hadn't seen her, or any other woman for that matter, since his foiled debauchery. This was worrisome since in his pursuit of Teache, not one day had passed, except when he was out to sea of course, that the scoundrel hadn't kept the company of at least one woman. Abnormal behavior was never a good sign.

Teache had also been riding hard without rest, so he had a purpose for this journey.

Abe covered his eyes as lightning flashed and it began to rain. "Blast," he uttered to the horse. It would be near impossible to keep up, if this turned into a squall.

Constanza entered her brother's bedroom and gently shook him.

"Will, wake up. I have to go and tend to the slaves in their quarters. Wake up now. Here is the musket. I want you and Ben to go and sit by the fire 'til I return. It should not be long. Bolt the door behind me."

Will sat up, rubbing his eyes. "Stanzy, what's going on?'

"I do not know, but you do not open for anyone except Lucian or me. Understood?"

Quickly quitting the cottage, she splashed through the muck and felt the cold water shoot under her dress and down into her boots as the rain began to fall sidelong in sheets.

"The place is cursed, ma'am," yelled Alphonse over the wind. "Almost everyone is sick, and some of the animals, they are dying, too. It is because of Mr. Hopkins being in league with the devil himself!"

"You mean Edward Teache? I know he is wicked, Alphonse, but I hardly think he is Lucifer in human form."

"I been hearing stories down in the towns of Teache's comings and goings. There is not an ounce of good in the man, far as I can tell, especially after all he has put this farm through. I am telling you I have been on this earth nearly eighty years and that man is pure evil."

Stanzy said nothing. She believed there was definitely a God, and there was definitely evil as well in the world. Her doubts as to her own sanity and reasoning ability continued. Could a place really be cursed?

She hurried to keep up with Alphonse as the rain poured on and on. When they finally reached the slave quarters the first word that entered her mind when she unbolted the door wasn't curse, but *plague*.

Everyone was either throwing up or their hands were violently shaking, Many covered their ears at the sound of the creaking door.

"Something is making everyone sick. They are not cursed," she said to Alphonse.

She bent over a smallish boy, Joseph, a little younger than Will. He was shaking more violently than the adults, and his eyes reminded her of something important, but she couldn't put her finger on it.

"Joseph, can you hear me?" She gently lifted him.

His mother lay close by on a cot and opened her eyes at the sound of his name. Her hands shook as well, and her lips mouthed silent words, but no sound issued forth.

Constanza sat beside her and cradled her hand in her own. The woman motioned for Stanzy to come closer and she leaned down to hear her whispers.

"Save my boy, Miss Stanzy."

She squeezed the woman's hand tight, pressed her lips together and nodded.

"Write this word on the door and let no one enter." She handed Alphonse a slip of paper: QUARANTINE.

Sick at heart, she opened the door and strode toward the barn. Upon entering, she put her hand over her nose to ward off the stench. Something squished underfoot. Several slaves knelt beside numerous dead carcasses of cows and sheep which were already rotting. She glanced down to see what she'd stepped on and her breath caught. Two of the pups from the litter lay dead on the hay-covered floor, next to the yellowed water in their bowl.

"Megan didn't kill her pup. The water did."

Then it dawned on her...the yellow water.

A hazy guess was forming in her mind and she ran toward the house in the driving rain. She looked into the air and saw that the sky was red, and inadvertently made a sound.

Unconsciously quoting the Bible, she said under her breath, "And in the morning, it will be foul weather today; for the sky is red and lowering."

She ran full tilt to the main house. Unable to maintain her balance, she skidded and fell in the water. The wind played tug-of-war with a massive bough, until it splintered with a resounding crack, like a wishbone. It winged directly toward her head. Dropping with her face in her hands, it sailed over, narrowly missing her.

"I hope tornadoes don't lead the way," she murmured.

She knew from experience the power of twisters that could arrive before or after the hurricanes on the coast. She uttered a soft prayer against the elements.

She scrambled up and headed for the cellar entrance to the house. Her eyes took a moment to adjust to the dim light. At least one hundred barrels sat on the dirt floor, some cracked opened, and some sealed shut. Moving from one to another, she searched until she found an empty one—one like those being used to store water for the manor and for the livestock.

With a trembling hand she scooped some of the water out and held it up to the candlelight. Sure enough, it had a faint yellow glint that was so slight it wouldn't be perceptible in the barrel.

"It is the water. There is something in the water from these barrels. They are contaminated."

That was the last thought she had before a beam struck her head and she collapsed like a rag-doll to the dirt floor.

The hurricane winds bore down full force on the Outer Banks. Lucian lowered his head against the pounding rain as he rode on toward Hyde County. His coat provided little protection as his water-soaked clothing clung to his skin. He kicked the skittish horse hard and urged her on, encouraging her to stay the course despite the storm.

News of the approaching storm had been circulating, and he'd started for home as soon as the words were out of the sailor's mouth. It wasn't the only thing about which the old tar had been telling tales. He'd told him about the now infamous Blackbeard the Pirate, whom Lucian could only assume was none other than their very own Edward Teache.

Lucian wondered on the whereabouts of Abe

Hornigold and wished he knew how to locate the man.

When the plantation came into view, he fought down the fear rising in his gut. As he watched, ancient trees were hoisted from the soil like saplings, and loose boards on the manor were flying into the air in all directions. The nearby river had flooded its banks and he feared it would flow the whole way to the farm.

Driving the mount on, he arrived at the cottage, halting and sliding from the saddle in one motion. He threw open the door.

"Ben! Will! Where are you?"

The boys yelled from under the floorboards. "Pa! We are down here!"

"Thank you," he whispered under his breath. "Where is your mother?"

Will's voice started to crack. "She left about an hour ago. Something is wrong with the slaves and the animals. She hasn't been back since!"

Fate kicked him hard in the stomach.

No. It would not happen again. He wouldn't let it.

"Go to the main house, and get in the root cellar. It is deeper. Go! Run!"

He shot out toward the slaves' cabin and stopped dead at the sign on the porch which read Quarantine. Someone had placed it half under a barrel in an attempt to keep it from blowing away. He kicked the front door which rocked open and shut before its hinges gave way, sending it flying up into the gale.

He entered and called, "Bess! Alphonse!"

They too had retreated under the floorboards to the root cellar. He opened the door in the floor and Bess stood on the steps looking up at him, near tears.

"Lucian, they is all sick, and now this Cane! I don't know how we will keep them all safe down here!"

"Where is Constanza?"

"Last time I saw her she was headed to the barn."

"Stay down there, Bess. We have rode out worse storms than this one. I will be back." He ran toward the main house, mechanically dodging the flying debris barreling through the air.

The manor contained three cellars, the root cellar, a food cellar and what he now called the rum cellar. He knew the family would either be in the food or root cellar, as Hopkins had been able to hide the rumrunning from Sarah up until now.

He slipped on the rain-covered steps leading to the rum cellar, landing with a crunch on his knees.

Panic, raw enough to make his head spin, made him lose focus. His eyes squinted to adjust to the dark as he bellowed, "Constanza! Constanza, you answer me right now!"

He shot down the barrel rows, his head whipping back and forth in all directions.

Where was she?

And then he saw her.

She was sprawled between two barrels, her head lying in a circular pool of blood. Her long hair drenched crimson.

"No...no, no, no..." Dropping to a knee beside her, he lifted her gently into his arms.

A ceiling beam lay nearby. He presumed it must have fallen on her.

"Stanzy, please. Oh, have mercy, please." He put his hand to her chest, and felt her heart beating strongly. She shivered from the cold.

"Lucian?" she said groggily.

"Yes, darling, it's me. You're going to be all right. We have to get out of here, into the other cellars."

"Lucian, the water is making everyone sick. It is why Meg is sick."

"All right, darling. We will take care of it." What was she talking about? Had the beam muddled her thinking momentarily?

"Lucian, do not patronize me!" She sat bolt upright out of his arms. With one hand she wiped at the blood on her face. She froze to examine his expression. He was smiling.

"You are unbelievable," he said. "Let's go. I don't want to die in the middle of this cursed rum."

"Lucian? What about Megan?"

"Oh, no. Come on." He half dragged her up the steps into the swirling winds.

They struggled to run against the driving rain. The tempest pushed them about like leaves in a gale. He opened the second storm cellar doors and peered into the gloom, searching for what he already knew in his heart wouldn't be there.

His little girl.

Unable to hide his panic, Lucian demanded of Hopkins. "Where is she?"

"It is a lost cause I am afraid, the top of the second floor has already been whipped away, there is no way she could have survived," was his flat answer.

"You didn't even look for her? Your own child?" shrieked Stanzy. Sarah stood cowering behind her useless husband.

Stanzy's hair, matted with blood, flung crimson droplets in all directions as she shook her head in disbelief. Their sickening spattered pattern dotted the floor beneath her.

They didn't need to exchange words, Lucian grabbed her hand and they bounded up the steps once again.

The sight in front of them was daunting. A large hunk of roof lay on the manor lawn, blocking their way. Heading around it, they stopped in shock. The remaining rooftop rose and fell, flapping in the wind as if the storm had breathed the house to life.

Cautiously, they entered through the front door. It would do no one any good for them to run headlong without thinking. The main entrance to the manor had caved in and the grand staircase was blocked with debris and rubble.

Stanzy could barely hear, the storm outside wailed like a banshee come to claim her victims. Lucian muttered something imperceptible that was whisked away on the howling wind. The only thing she could see was his mouth moving, forming the words, "Please, no..."

He pulled her behind him to the kitchen.

Opening the door to the back stairwell revealed it too had been partially damaged. They began digging furiously through the mounds of splintered wood. A thunderous sound from behind made them involuntarily cover their heads as a tree limb crashed through the window in the kitchen, sending glass slicing in all directions.

"Dig!" Lucian bellowed above the din.

Stanzy dug both hands into the pile, weeping hysterically. Her mind felt rent in two at the horrible sadness of it all. It was ready to snap, and if it did, she would never be the same again. Clearing a very small space to see up the staircase, it was obvious which one of them would need to enter the fallen stairwell.

"Go find her. Hurry! I am sure the eye of the storm will be here at any minute."

Lucian hoisted her up and she slid through the top of the pile of rubble. The scene at the top of the stairs gave her pause. Half of Megan's roof was blown away. The gaping hole resembled a yawning mouth; blackened storm clouds swirled directly above in the night sky. Smaller pieces of furniture took flight, revolving slowly in the updraft, whisking out the hole into the tornado. Her dolls rose in the air in a macabre waltz, before they too careened out of sight through the open ceiling.

Stanzy crawled her way over downed planks and tree boughs littering the nursery floor. Water poured in from the sky in a deluge, as if the heavens had opened for a second time to allow a second flooding of the earth. The tempest seemed poised just above the mansion.

Megan's heavy wardrobe still stood in the corner of the room, albeit it had moved a few feet. Frantically searching about the room, Megan was nowhere in sight.

Where are you? Where are you? Please Megan...

Stanzy fought her way toward the huge cabinet and tugged at its monstrous doors. They wouldn't budge. She furiously looked around the room for something with which to pry them open, but everything useful was gone from the room.

Then she heard it. Whimpering from inside the

wardrobe. *Thank you, God!*

Constanza screamed into the wind. "We are here Megan, we are coming!"

The doors rattled as Megan's tiny fists pummeled against it.

Stanzy made her way back across the debris to the hole. She yelled down to Lucian, "I can't get into her wardrobe, find me something to pry it open!"

Lucian scrambled around the kitchen and could find nothing useful. He opened the door to the outside and it flew off into the gale immediately. On the ground lay an axe embedded in the dirt, which he grabbed, ran back to the stairwell and proceeded to shove it through the hole.

Stanzy snatched the long handle and when she reached the wardrobe screamed, "Megan. Move as far into the corner as you can and stay perfectly still." She was all too aware if Megan didn't heed her, she might kill or maim her forever, but what choice did she have? They may all three be dead in a minute if the eye of the tornado touched down close enough to the manor.

She smashed the door with the axe and it barely cracked. It was thick and old. She whacked it again and again. Pure unadulterated rage overtook her. Through her mind raced pictures of injustice—her drunken father; the face of Megan, who hadn't asked to be ill, mute and left for dead; the faces of the innocent patients she'd seen die horrid deaths.

And it cracked.

Just before her mind did.

She threw the axe aside and peered into the wardrobe.

There she sat. Beautiful little Megan curled up in a ball in the corner. "Oh, Megan!"

"Mama! Ma! Please! Please!" Megan scampered across the floor of the wardrobe into Stanzy's outstretched arms.

Fervently hugging her close for a precious few seconds, Stanzy gathered her up, making her way back to the stairs. Carefully, she dropped Megan through the hole into Lucian's outstretched arms.

~ *Chapter Fifteen* ~

Once dealing its monstrous devastation, the maelstrom passed—rain ceased and winds calmed. Hopkins sat at Lucian's kitchen table. Damage to the cottage was minimal compared to the manor, which was almost a total loss. It would take at least a year to rebuild. Crops had been partially destroyed, but some would be salvageable.

After staring at the tabletop as Lucian and Stanzy waited, he finally looked up. "I have discussed it with Sarah, and we feel it is in Megan's best interests for her to stay with you, and let you adopt her as your child." His voice caught and choked. "Sarah wants to leave here...go to town. So, we are moving to Bath and do not feel it would be an appropriate place for...for a child like her."

Predictably, Lucian squeezed Stanzy's hand under the table to stay her mouth, in his anticipation she would blurt out something to the tune of how Meg was just a burden to them. But though she believed that true, she was actually sighing with relief at this revelation.

For once, Lucian was wrong about her reaction. Now that she was certain Meg was to stay with them, she would take no risk that might jeopardize the adoption.

"I also have the papers, entitling you to the land you were promised, and you are free from my employ."

"Good luck, Ian," Lucian said, extending his hand.

"You are a good man, Lucian," he said in return and headed out the door without a backward glance.

The second the door shut, Stanzy flung herself into his arms. "She is ours."

"There is only one more thing I require to make this family complete," he said, looking into the room where Will and Ben sat on the floor with Megan.

Tears of joy clouded her vision as she looked into his face. "And what would that be, dear husband?"

"One more girl, preferably with your eyes, and *my* temperament."

She slapped him hard on the arm.

With all the rebuilding under way, the week after the storm passed quickly.

One-time slaves were now employed by Lucian as free workers, and the restoration of StoneWater was going smoothly.

Lucian kept his promise with regard to trying for a little girl to add to their brood. It seemed he couldn't keep his breeches on for any length of time. He was happier than Stanzy had ever seen him when he left for the port to restock their destroyed stores. He turned in the wagon to smile and wave his hat at her as he wound his way out of the estate.

Later, with the arrival of dusk, she stood on the porch squinting to make out the approaching horseman.

The rider carrying the mail pouch dismounted and strode toward the cottage. "Mrs. Blackwell?"

"Yes?"

"This letter is for you. I am afraid it was delayed by the storm."

He wasn't even off the porch before she had it torn open.

Katrina's handwriting, which she barely recognized, was forced and almost illegible.

"Dear Stanzy,

"By the time you read this, you may call me Mrs. Teache. I have resolved to marry Edward and invite you to come to our home at Hammock House as soon as you are able. You were such a fool to have turned him down, but no matter, for now he is mine!

"I hope to see you soon. I often think of our days together on the voyage from England and the lucky girls who linked themselves to sailors on that voyage! Now I am one of them!"

"Your dearest,

"Katrina"

"Heavens be merciful," was all Stanzy uttered, and within a quarter hour she was en route to Hammock House.

Lucian sat at the bar in Nags Head and ordered ale for the cheery, albeit drunk, Abernathy Hornigold.

"So you think you have him?" said Lucian, almost as bleary eyed.

"Yes, it should all end very soon, and I will be free to return home to my family! Everything has come to a head with his latest marriage to a young beauty named Katrina. By my ciphering, his twelfth or thirteenth wife."

Lucian spewed the beer in his mouth onto the bar.

Stanzy had ridden through the night, refusing to stop. Taylor Creek was now in sight, so she knew the pirate's cottage was close. Hammock House was located somewhere along the river. Astride her mount, she scanned the countryside with squinted eyes.

Her breath hitched in her throat at the sight. Situated high on a knoll, it wasn't the white house itself which caught her eye. A young girl was swinging from a noose on a tree in front of the dwelling; her body flowed in time with the gently blowing breeze.

Drawing her rifle, she kicked the horse on, offering a silent prayer that she wasn't pregnant, and about to get two people killed instead of one. Dismounting, she skulked toward the house, skirting from one tree to the next. Crumpling, she grabbed hold of the tree for support; her legs shook so violently, she wasn't sure she could walk, let alone rescue Katrina. She snuck again to the tree nearest the house. Her hands shook as she prepped the rifle. Carefully, she ticked off the steps with Uncle Delvin's voice as her guide, so that the lead didn't become stuck in the barrel and blow up in her hands.

Her Uncle Delvin's instructions came to her then— her mind's eye picturing his massive gentle hands lifting the rifle to its proper height. She raised the end of the musket and looked through the sights as she whispered in her mind: *The higher the angle of the rifle, the longer the trajectory.*

She snuck up behind the tree where the young girl was hanging and closed her eyes for a minute before looking up. A mixture of revulsion and relief washed over her when she realized it wasn't Katrina.

The poor girl had been lovely, and of a foreign descent Stanzy was unable to pinpoint. And very much pregnant. For a moment it didn't register and then it shook her to the core...it was the woman who had accused Lucian of infidelity. Teache had been behind the charade all along, and this poor creature had been his pawn. She quickly said a prayer for her and continued on toward Hammock House.

Stealthily, she moved around the back of the house and peered in a window. Not a soul was in sight. As quietly as possible, she turned the handle and slowly pushed the door open. Still seeing no one, she slid in and tiptoed through the kitchen, stopping and cocking her head to the side, straining to hear any voices or sounds.

She searched the entire downstairs, then looked up the stairwell. If she went up, and if there were more than one man, she would be trapped. But what choice did she have? Katrina, the fool, was undoubtedly here.

With her gun held at the ready, she ascended the staircase. When she reached the landing at the top, her heart sank. In the room to her left was Katrina, bound and gagged.

Their eyes met briefly and Stanzy stepped toward her. Katrina shook her head back and forth, her eyes widening in horror. No!

Click.

Stanzy turned to face Teache, towering over her with his pistol cocked, pointed at her temple.

"Allo, beautiful. Did you like our letter? Come to bring us a weddin' gift? Let us head down the stairs to the porch. You will love the view."

With the pistol to the back of her head, he wrenched the rifle from her fingertips and guided her roughly by the elbow down the stairs and out onto the porch.

"Search 'er. I am sure the clever lass has come prepared."

A sailor smiled, revealing blackened teeth. His breath stank of old ale as he groped in search of any concealed weapons. He found and removed a knife she'd strapped to the inside of her thigh. The sneer he gave as he extracted it sickened her.

Constanza said nothing, but counted the number of seamen she could see—fifteen in all.

"Ever since I first laid eyes on you, I knew I must have you. And when you showed such dislike for me, it made me all the more determined to have my way. Let me explain it to you plain like..." Teache leered within an inch of her face. She could see the black in his teeth, and the smell of him was soured ale. He continued, "We can do this the easy way or the hard way. You see, all I have ever wanted was you, Constanza, not the spoiled, whining princess tied to the chair upstairs. The likes of her is a dime a dozen; but you...you are the real treasure. I can either take her chastity, then kill both of you, or *you* can give yourself willingly to me, and your sister will go free."

A disembodied feeling overtook her as if she merely observed from afar. Her mind splintered like shattered glass as it tried in vain to find an alternate reality than the one laid at her feet.

Lucian's beautiful face came to mind, and she felt shame at the act she must consent to—to save them.

"Let her go. I want to watch her get on a horse and ride away before you—" But she vomited before she could finish.

Everything around her was cloudy. Putting her hands to her head, she tried to focus, but her mind refused. Her faculties felt bludgeoned; Teache had stolen something from her soul that could not be retrieved. No amount of time would heal this damage to her spirit.

He is pure evil...and I've lain with him.

Wild images kept firing in her mind, and the realization she must be hallucinating dawned on her. In every direction, wailing women in ripped white dresses pulled their hair out. To her right, a blonde in a tattered dress, to her left women who looked like gypsies. She was unsure whether they were real or not. Then she saw fairies soaring through the canopy of the cypress trees... beautiful women with wings, all crying as they stared at her. Their tears burned as they hit her flesh. And millions of fireflies seemed to have appeared out of nowhere. They lit up the path on which she plodded along.

Hallucinations. I have passed into the world of my grandmother.

Collapsing to her knees on the roadside, her gut contracted and she retched. Relenting, she quit the fight and vomited, again and again.

Memories her mind only permitted in the form of dreams began to break their way through into her conscious mind.

"Come here, poppet. You know that all I teach you is a rare privilege for a woman, but I think we both know you are no ordinary woman. You would never be satisfied with needlework and mending and cooking. I know the thoughts in that head of yours."

Constanza obediently came closer to the recently dead body. This is the perfect time to review the musculature of the arm.

The man had been in a carriage accident—crushed by the weight of the carriage. Her father had done what he could, but the poor man was almost dead when he arrived in their office.

His arm was torn open at the forearm. It lay palm up on the table. Her father used the other end of the scalpel to lift each individual muscle from its resting location.

"Here is flexor digitorum superficialis," he said, concurrently pulling at the muscles to flex all of the

fingers.

"This other below it, is the profundus, which I cannot reach without removing these. Also, very important is almaris longus. This is an extra muscle, not everyone has it, but fortunately for you, this man does, or did. What a great opportunity for you. I know you are not the least bit artistic, but quickly draw yourself a sketch for future reference, and add it to your notes.

"Someday you will thank me for this."

"Ha. Yes, thank you, Father. Every sixteen-year-old wants to see a cadaver's muscles."

The sound of her giggling sent gooseflesh erupting up her arms.

Like little rips in a curtain where daylight peeks through, little bits of memories slipped out from their protected spots. She was at their mercy now.

The face of the first woman that passed during childbirth appeared before her. Faces of all the dead who'd been lost on her father's operating table—the old man with the blackened, infected leg, each level of amputation failed, and they sawed, and sawed. A young woman driven to madness, who no longer spoke, but only sang haunting songs. The upturned faces of the babes she'd carried through the snow to the orphanage, their eyes regarding her with all of the faith in the world...so much suffering.

Still on her knees, her head felt thick and heavy with the memories and she let it droop into her hands. She muttered, "No more suffering, please, please. No more."

She rose to her feet. After a while, she vaguely registered her feet were raw and rubbed bloody, due to the rain. When had it started? She spied Taylor Creek over the hill to her right and started down the slope toward the water.

Trudging down the slope, her feet slid in the thick mud, and she made no attempt to stop her descent. In fact she welcomed it. She threw her arms wide. *Enough of this torture called life.*

Torture in the fact that anyone or anything she ever cared about had either been desecrated or died before her very eyes.

As she slid, she felt the stones rip at her back and head, but she cared not. She lay stone still, the freezing stream rising up her legs. If she refused to move, she would probably go under. The rain poured full force now and she opened her eyes and stared into the canopy of trees. Her entire body shook, almost like Megan's in the throes of a fit.

Megan.

Lucian.

Will.

Ben.

They needed her. And if she died, what would become of them?

Her mind filled with thoughts of Megan, again.

Megan...the child who called her mother—a word she never thought to hear or want to hear in her life. She'd sworn that if she reared her brother and sister safely, she would never tie herself down to any responsibility again.

But love isn't interested in responsibility.

Now she understood how you could adopt a child in your heart, and if you truly loved that child, it was as if you had brought him or her forth from your own body.

This was how she loved Megan. And she now realized the extent of the love she had for Will and, yes, even Katrina, and especially Lucian. She would die for any one of them if it came to it. She loved them as she loved her own flesh. Who else would love them that way, if she permitted this surreal reality to take her mind? Who would be brave enough to fight for them every day?

No one.

There were still principles worth fighting for.

She fought the blackness attempting to close her eyes, never to open them again.

Sudden anger blazed violently, and she knew if that devil Teache were in front of her she would be capable of murder. Anger, not only for herself, but also for that pitiful creature swinging in the wind in front of Hammock House. And for who knows how many children and women Teache had fooled and abandoned. Anger for her own lost childhood, her foolish mother, and her irresponsible father who had subjected her to pain and abuse that *no child* should ever have to bear.

The desire to return home blazed within her...but not with the stench of him still clinging to her. She refused to contaminate her home with his reeking funk. She climbed full into the freezing stream and began to scrub. With all her might, she tried to wash *him* off of her. She came back to her senses when she saw blood trickling down her arm. She'd scrubbed her skin until she bled.

Slowly she stood and made her way up the hillside to the road. Horses were coming...she could hear them... but didn't bother to get out of the way. Trampling would be preferable. She had to quit thinking like this.

The animals halted before her. Sitting astride them were Katrina, Lucian, and a man she'd never seen, as well as several others she vaguely recognized to be sailors. They dismounted.

"Stanzy, are you all right? Are you...intact?"

Intact?

Even as Lucian spoke the words, his face worked as if he might go mad. His contorted face looked as if the end of all things had arrived.

He knows. I do not even have to tell him.

Stanzy's eyes met Katrina's as she spoke, recognizing the same flat tones her mother had used when spilling lies. Stanzy looked at Lucian and said, "I escaped, darling, out the window, and they have all departed in their sloop out into the inlet."

Stanzy sat staring out the window of the cottage, waiting for Lucian to return from the barn. The last nine months had slipped past, quiet and calm. Their homestead was finished, and Katrina had finally found love—hopefully for real this time. And to whom else but a sailor—the eldest son of one Abernathy Hornigold.

Their mother had always said, "You reap what you sow."

The fall of Edward Teache at Ocracoke Inlet on 22 November, and how it had been a gruesome battle, was the talk of every town on the Banks. Two small sloops, the *Ranger* and *Jane*, leased personally by Governor Spottswood, had finally caught up to the devil, thanks to the recommendations of Hornigold. The larger, military ships wouldn't have been quick enough to catch Teache.

Purportedly, he'd received multiple musket shots, and no less than twenty slices of a blade before going down for good. He was then beheaded and his head taken aboard the ship. It was said that his corpse swam the length of the boats three times before disappearing into the watery depths.

Maybe he had been real evil.

At times, she found herself shaking when all around her was peaceful, and at other times, any strong emotion could elicit irrational fear. A hot flush of heat to the side of her face ensued, and her heart raced as if she were in fear for her life. And she rarely slept, because at night the dreams were full of filthy pirates, lost babies and dead mothers with vacant eyes.

Her nightmares over the past nine months arrived from the moment she closed her eyes, until she woke sweat covered and shaking every morn. Her mind felt like splintered glass, just one sudden jolt might send it disintegrating into a million tiny bits.

The mother's belly contracts as she howls in pain. Stanzy pushes down as she has a thousand times before, but nothing happens. It is not coming. She gets behind the woman and heaves her upright to speed the labor, but the wailing continues. Smells issue forth, not common to a delivery room—sulphur and gunpowder. The walls of the delivery room rip away like the sides of the manor in the hurricane, and in their stead is the horizon, and ships. Ships flying black flags of skeletons in different forms.

They are coming for her, the Brethren of the Coast, and there is nothing she can do about it. And she knows she will have to sail with them forever. She will not even have the peace of death.

The horizon is red and the sea churns with creatures. Not the creatures she so dearly loves, but horned, scaled creatures of unknown names that slink in and out of the depths, begging her to throw herself overboard. Then mermaids with pointed, razor sharp teeth that they open and close, gnashing them at her.

The woman yells again.

Stanzy stumbles to the bottom of the bed to try to deliver the child. But something is wrong; the woman's water breaks and spills over the table, but it isn't amniotic fluid, it is seawater. The baby is delivered into her hands and its tiny body is covered in black hair. And as she looks at the face of the woman on the table for the first time she sees her own face staring back at her.

Night after night, the dream recurs, and she cannot escape it, awake or asleep. She prays that when the baby is born, whomever the father, that the cursed dream will cease, and permit her some peace.

Stanzy ran her hands over her pregnant belly. Suddenly her water broke. Icy fear, instead of elation filled her. She prayed that when she looked upon this child, the hair would be brown, and his soul would be the salt of the earth, and not the son of the devil with a longing for the sea.

~ *Epilogue* ~

The baby cried as Lucian handed him to Stanzy. Tears streaked down her face blurring her vision as she cradled him to her breast. She took a wet cloth and began to swab his hair—fine, brown hair. When his tiny eyes met hers, she recognized the exact beautiful hazel color which met her own gaze each and every morning.

Lucian's eyes.

She knew now she would be able to tell him the truth of what transpired at Hammock House and perhaps with that real healing could begin. All was forgiven. The baby was what they had wished for, a beautiful boy in whom their love could continue on for generations.

"He's perfect, Stanzy. He'll have your hair." Lucian bent and encircled the two of them.

Love beat back the demons raging in her head. A single beam of sunlight shone through the window, recalling one word to her mind.

Hope.

As she slept, for the first time in almost a year, no creatures plagued her sleep. Only green fields where four children frolicked, chasing one another's shadows.

Author's Notes

Lead Poisoning in the 1700s

As the parent of a child who has suffered lead poisoning, as well as other metal toxicities, I have seen the devastating effects of this problem firsthand. Symptoms of lead and mercury toxicity can be malaise, gastrointestinal problems, nephritis (kidney disease), and in extreme cases...convulsions, pica (eating non-food substances), paralysis and death.

In 1786, Benjamin Franklin wrote a letter to the political economist Benjamin Vaughan, in which he related recollections from his boyhood. At that time, Franklin recalled legal cases involving New England rum, where distributors had used leaden still-heads and worms in casks, and the lead had leached into the rum, causing illness and paralysis. The Legislature of Massachusetts enacted laws prohibiting this practice. Franklin also discussed the case of a family that had consumed rainwater, which had passed over their roof and had been caught in barrels, and were affected by lead poisoning. Thus the barrel in our story was lead laden...as well as the lack of moss on the roof, which could not grow due to lead as well.

Blackbeard's Wives

The only account on record that I was able to locate on Blackbeard's documented marriage was to a Mary Ormond from Bath. It is said that Blackbeard would go into ports and find the most desirable women, take them aboard his ship, and have one of his crewmen marry them. This happened so often, it was common-place for his crew!

In the town of Beaufort, North Carolina, there is

actually a walking tour you can take of Hammock House, and Blackbeard was rumored to have hanged one of his wives on a tree from a noose until dead (TourBeaufort.com). Hammock House was indeed at one time the home of Blackbeard, the time and circumstances are purely a product of the author's imagination, however.

I encourage one and all to visit the Outer Banks of North Carolina if you are a history buff, as the entire coast is steeped in tradition and folklore. It is breathtakingly beautiful.

US COAST GUARD

Lucian's father, who drowned in a rescue mission offshore, was created in this writer's imagination, but it is a matter of record that many truly brave souls have rescued stranded passengers for as long as the Outer Banks have been inhabited.

The Chicamacomico Lifesaving Station was in operation from 1874 to 1915 and was a precursor to the Coast Guard, which began around 1918.

Tactile Defensiveness

The behaviors of Megan—the inability to tolerate clothing, or having one's hair washed or brushed or nails cut—is very much a reality in many disorders. It results from improper nerve transmission to a person's skin, so they either react too much or too little to touch.

The exceedingly high pain tolerance is a reality as well—the author has witnessed children pound their heads on tile floors and never shed a single tear.

Tribute

Although the rape scene with regard to Katrina and Stanzy is a part of my fictitious novel, I have known in my lifetime a real story of rape, where one brave soul indeed took another's place and endured the torture of this deed to preserve the innocence of a loved one...the telling of this tale is a tribute to that brave and courageous person. There are few like you on the earth today.

About the Author

Brynn Chapman

Born in Pennsylvania and raised by two school teacher parents, Brynn loved reading and writing from an early age. After reading *The Lord of the Rings* for the first time when 13 years old, she was henceforth fixated on all fantasy stories and folklore.

Concerned over the practicality of becoming a writer when college bound, Brynn decided on a medical career instead of a literary one. As she grew older, the artistic side of her brain would not be silenced, so she returned to her first love—writing.

Brynn still resides in Penn's Woods with her husband and three sons. She also works as an occupational therapist for children with autism and at a charter school for adolescents on the spectrum.

She is also the author of the young adult fantasy, *Into the Woods*, written as R.R. Smythe.

Also Available from Highland Press

Katherine Deauxville
Southern Fried Trouble

Deborah MacGillivray
Cat O'Nine Tales

Leanne Burroughs
Highland Wishes

Ashley Kath-Bilsky
The Sense of Honor

Isabel Mere
Almost Taken

Isabel Mere
Almost Guilty

R.R. Smythe
Into the Woods
(A Young Adult Fantasy)

Leanne Burroughs
Her Highland Rogue

Jacquie Rogers
Faery Special Romances

Rebecca Andrews
The Millennium Phrase Book

Chris Holmes
Blood on the Tartan

Jean Harrington
The Barefoot Queen

Anne Kimberly
Dark Well of Decision

Young/Ivey/Chai
Brides of the West

Candace Gold
A Heated Romance
Jo Webnar
Saving Tampa
Diane Davis White
Moon of Falling Leaves
Eric Fullilove
The Zero Day Event
Molly Zenk
Chasing Byron
Katherine Deauxville
The Crystal Heart
Cynthia Owens
In Sunshine or In Shadow
Jannine Corti Petska
Rebel Heart
Phyllis Campbell
Pretend I'm Yours
Holiday Romance Anthology
Christmas Wishes
Holiday Romance Anthology
Holiday in the Heart
Romance Anthology
No Law Against Love
Romance Anthology
Blue Moon Magic
Romance Anthology
Blue Moon Enchantment
Romance Anthology
Recipe for Love
Holiday Romance Anthology
Love Under the Mistletoe
Holiday Romance Anthology
Romance Upon A Midnight Clear

Upcoming

Lance Martin
The Little Hermit
(Children's Illustrated)
John Nieman & Karen Laurence
The Amazing Rabbitini
(Children's Illustrated)
Dawn Thompson
Rape of the Soul
Jacquie Rogers
Down Home Ever Lovin' Mule Blues
Romance Anthology
No Law Against Love 2
Romance Anthology
Second Time Around
Romance Anthology
The Way to a Man's Heart
Romance Anthology
Love on a Harley
*Wildes/MacGillivray/Breeding/
Young/Burroughs*
Castle of Dreams
*MacGillivray/Burroughs/
Bowen/Houseman*
Dance en L'Aire
Sorter/MacGillivray/Burroughs
Faith, Hope and Redemption
Linda Bilodeau
The Wine Seekers
Sandra Cox
The Sundial
Judith Leigh
When the Vow Breaks

Freddie Currie
The Changing Wind
Anne Holman
The Master of Strathgian
Amber Dawn Bell
Cave of Terror – Chronicles of a Vampire Gymnast
Cleora Comer
Just DeEtta
Judith Leigh
Joshua's Faith
Don Brookes
With Silence and Tears
Romance Anthology
Love and Glory
Jeanmarie Hamilton
Seduction
Jean Drew
Eternal Hearts
Katherine Shaw
Love Thy Neighbor
Judith Leigh
A Father's Hope
Jean Harrington
In the Lion's Mouth
Inspirational Romance Anthology
The Miracle of Love
Chris Holmes
The Mosquito Tapes
Jean Drew
Beats A Wild Heart
Isabel Mere
Almost Silenced
Judith Leigh/Cheryl Norman

Route 66
Dawn Thompson
Odin's Daughter
Dawn Thompson
Children of the Wind
Dawn Thompson
Drake's Lair
Katherine Deauxville
Enraptured
Katherine Deauxville
Eyes of Love

*Check our website frequently for
future releases.*

www.highlandpress.org

Brynn Chapman

Praise for more Highland Press Books!

THE CRYSTAL HEART by Katherine Deauxville brims with ribald humor and authentic historical detail. Enjoy!

~ *Virginia Henley*

* * *

CAT O'NINE TALES by Deborah MacGillivray. Enchanting tales from the most wicked, award-winning author today. Spellbinding! A treat for all.

~ *Detra Fitch, The Huntress Reviews*

* * *

HIGHLAND WISHES by Leanne Burroughs. This reviewer found that this book was a wonderful story set in a time when tension was high between England and Scotland. She writes a well-crafted story, with multidimensional characters and exquisite backdrops of Scotland. The storyline is a fast-paced tale with much detail to specific areas of history. The reader can feel this author's love for Scotland and its many wonderful heroes.

This reviewer was easily captivated by the story and was enthralled by it until the end. The reader will laugh and cry as you read this wonderful story. The reader feels all the pain, torment and disillusionment felt by both main characters, but also the joy and love they felt. Ms. Burroughs has crafted a well-researched story that gives a glimpse into Scotland during a time when there was upheaval and war for independence. This reviewer is anxiously awaiting her next novel in this series and commends her for a wonderful job done.

~*Dawn Roberto, Love Romances*

* * *

THE SENSE OF HONOR by Ashley Kath-Bilsky has written an historical romance of the highest caliber. This reviewer was fesseled to the pages, fell in love with the hero and was cheering for the heroine all the way through. The plot is exciting and moves along at a good pace. The characters are multi-dimensional and the secondary characters bring life to the story. Sexual tension rages through this story and Ms. Kath-Bilsky gives her readers a breath-taking romance. The love scenes are sensual and very romantic. This reviewer was very pleased with how the author handled all the secrets. Sometimes it can be very frustrating for the reader when secrets keep tearing the main characters apart, but in this case, those secrets seem to bring them more together and both characters reacted very maturely when the secrets finally came to light. This reviewer is hoping that this very talented author will have another book out very soon.

~ Valerie, Love Romances

* * *

FAERY SPECIAL ROMANCES - Brilliantly magical! Ms. Rogers' special brand of humor and imagination will have you believing in faeries from page one. Absolutely enchanting!

~ Dawn Thompson, Author of
The Ravencliff Bride

* * *

IN SUNSHINE OR IN SHADOW by Cynthia Owens - If you adore the stormy heroes of 'Wuthering Heights' and 'Jane Eyre' (and who doesn't?) you'll be entranced by Owens' passionate story of Ireland after the Great Famine, and David Burke - a man from America with a hidden past and a secret name. Only one woman, the fiery, luscious Siobhan, can unlock the bonds that imprison him. Highly recommended for those who love classic romance and an action-packed story.

~ Maggie Davis, AKA Katherine
Deauxville, Best Selling Author

* * *

INTO THE WOODS by R.R. Smythe - This Young Adult Fantasy will send chills down your spine. I, as the reader, followed Callum and witnessed everything he and his friends went through as they attempted to decipher the messages. At the same time, I watched Callum's mother, Ellsbeth, as she walked through the Netherwood. Each time Callum deciphered one of the four messages, some villagers awakened. Through the eyes of Ellsbeth, I saw the other sleepers wander, make mistakes, and be released from the Netherwood, leaving Ellsbeth alone. There is one thread left dangling, but do not fret. This IS a stand alone book. But that thread gives me hope that another book about the Netherwoods may someday come to pass. Excellent reading for any age of fantasy fans!

~ Detra Fitch, Huntress Reviews

* * *

ALMOST TAKEN by Isabel Mere is a very passionate historical romance that takes the reader on an exciting adventure. The compelling characters of Deran Morissey, the Earl of Atherton, and Ava Fychon, a young woman from Wales, find themselves drawn together as they search for her missing siblings.

Readers will watch in interest as they fall in love and overcome obstacles. They will thrill in the passion and hope that they find happiness together. This is a very sensual romance that wins the heart of the readers. This is a creative and fast moving storyline that will enthrall readers. The character's personalities will fascinate readers and win their concern. Ava, who is highly spirited and stubborn, will win the respect of the readers for her courage and determination. Deran, who is rumored in the beginning to be an ice king, not caring about anyone, will prove how wrong people's perceptions can be. **Almost Taken** by Isabel Mere is an emotionally moving historical romance that I highly recommend to the readers.

~ *Anita, The Romance Studio*

* * *

Leanne Burroughs easily will captivate the reader with intricate details, a mystery that ensnares the reader and characters that will touch their hearts. By the end of the first chapter, this reviewer was enthralled with **HER HIGHLAND ROGUE** and was rooting for Duncan and Catherine to admit their love. Laughter, tears and love shine through this wonderful novel. This reviewer was amazed at Ms. Burroughs' depth and perception in this storyline. Her wonderful way with words plays itself through each page like a lyrical note and will captivate the reader till the very end. The only drawback was this reviewer wanted to know more of the secondary characters and the back story of other characters. All in all, read HER HIGHLAND ROGUE and be transported to a time that is full of mystery and promise of a future. This reviewer is highly recommending this book for those who enjoy an engrossing Scottish tale full of humor, love and laughter.

~*Dawn Roberto, Love Romances*

* * *

PRETEND I'M YOURS by Phyllis Campbell is an exceptional masterpiece. This lovely story is so rich in detail and personalities that it just leaps out and grabs hold of the reader. From the moment I started reading about Mercedes and Katherine, I was spellbound. Ms. Campbell carries the reader into a mirage of mystery with deceit, betrayal of the worst kind, and a passionate love revolving around the sisters, that makes this a whirlwind page-turner. Mercedes and William are astonishing characters that ignite the pages and allows the reader to experience all their deepening sensations. There were moments I could share in with their breathtaking romance, almost feeling the butterflies of love they emitted. This extraordinary read had me

mesmerized with its ambiance, its characters and its remarkable twists and turns, making it one recommended read in my book.
~ *Linda L., Fallen Angel Reviews*

* * *

REBEL HEART by Jannine Corti Petska - Ms. Petska does an excellent job of all aspects of sharing this book with us. Ms. Petska used a myriad of emotions to tell this story and the reader (me) quickly becomes entranced in the ways Courtney's stubborn attitude works to her advantage in surviving this disastrous beginning to her new life. Ms. Petska's writings demand attention; she draws the reader to quickly become involved in this passionate story. This is a wonderful rendition of a different type which is a welcome addition to the historical romance genre. I believe that you will enjoy this story; I know I did!
~ *Brenda Talley, The Romance Studio*

* * *

BLOOD ON THE TARTAN by Chris Holmes is the powerful tale of a little known ugly time in Scotland, where raw, fighting Scottish spirit gathers itself to challenge injustice. In Catherine Ross and Ian Macgregor the reader is treated to a rare romance and love triumphant as they fight for Scottish honor.
~*Robert Middlemiss, A Common Glory*

* * *

BRIDES OF THE WEST by Michele Ann Young, Kimberly Ivey, and Billie Warren Chai - All three of the stories in this wonderful anthology are based on women who gambled their future in blindly accepting complete strangers for husbands. It was a different era when a woman must have a husband to survive and all three of these phenomenal authors wrote exceptional stories featuring fascinating and gutsy heroines and the men who loved them. For an engrossing read with splendid

original stories I highly encourage reader's to pick up a copy of this marvelous anthology.
~ *Marilyn Rondeau, Reviewers International Organization*

* * *

A HEATED ROMANCE - Author Candace Gold literally burns up the pages with this strong debut novel, marking her as a talent to watch.
Highly recommended.
~ *Dawn Thompson, author of The Ravencliff Bride*

* * *

RECIPE FOR LOVE - I don't think the reader will find a better compilation of mouth watering short romantic love stories than in RECIPE FOR LOVE! This is a highly recommended volume – perfect for beaches, doctor's offices, or anywhere you've a few minutes to read.
~ *Marilyn Rondeau, Reviewers International Organization*

* * *

Christmas is a magical time and twelve talented authors answer the question of what happens when **CHRISTMAS WISHES** come true in this incredible anthology.

Christmas Wishes shows just how phenomenal a themed anthology can be. Each of these highly skilled authors brings a slightly different perspective to the Christmas theme to create a book that is sure to leave readers satisfied. What a joy to read such splendid stories! This reviewer looks forward to more anthologies by Highland Press as the quality is simply astonishing.
~ *Debbie, CK2S Kwips and Kritiques*

* * *

HOLIDAY IN THE HEART - Twelve stories that would put even Scrooge into the Christmas spirit. It does not matter what *type* of romance genre you prefer. This book has a little bit of everything. The stories are set in the U.S.A. and Europe. Some take place in the past, some in the present, and one story takes place in both! I strongly suggest that you put on something comfortable, brew up something hot (tea, coffee or cocoa will do), light up a fire, settle down somewhere quiet and begin reading this anthology.

~ *Detra Fitch, Huntress Reviews*

* * *

BLUE MOON MAGIC is an enchanting collection of short stories. Each author wrote with the same theme in mind but each story has its own uniqueness. You should have no problem finding a tale to suit your mood. *BLUE MOON MAGIC* offers historicals, contemporaries, time travel, paranormal, and futuristic narratives to tempt your heart.

Legend says that if you wish with all your heart upon the rare blue moon, your wishes were sure to come true. Each of the heroines discovers this magical fact. True love is out there if you just believe in it. In some of the stories, love happens in the most unusual ways. Angels may help, ancient spells may be broken, anything can happen. Even vampires will find their perfect mate with the power of the blue moon. Not every heroine believes they are wishing for love, some are just looking for answers to their problems or nagging questions. Fate seems to think the solution is finding the one who makes their heart sing.

BLUE MOON MAGIC is a perfect read for late at night or even during your commute to work. The short yet sweet stories are a wonderful way to spend a few minutes. If you do not have the time to finish a full-length novel, but hate stopping in the middle of a loving tale, I highly recommend grabbing this book.

~ *Kim Swiderski, Writers*
Unlimited Reviewer

* * *

Legend has it that a blue moon is enchanted. What happens when fifteen talented authors utilize this theme to create enthralling stories of love?

BLUE MOON ENCHANTMENT is a wonderful, themed anthology filled with phenomenal stories by fifteen extraordinarily talented authors. Readers will find a wide variety of time periods and styles showcased in this superb anthology. *BLUE MOON ENCHANTMENT* is sure to offer a little something for everyone!
~ *Debbie, CK²S Kwips and Kritiques*

* * *

NO LAW AGAINST LOVE - If you have ever found yourself rolling your eyes at some of the more stupid laws, then you are going to adore this novel. Over twenty-five stories fill up this anthology, each one dealing with at least one stupid or outdated law. Let me give you an example: In Florida, USA, there is a law that states "If an elephant is left tied to a parking meter, the parking fee has to be paid just as it would for a vehicle." In Great Britain, "A license is required to keep a lunatic." Yes, you read those correctly. No matter how many times you go back and reread them, the words will remain the same. Those two laws are still legal. The tales vary in time and place. Some take place in the present, in the past, in the USA, in England...in other words, there is something for everyone! Best yet, profits from the sales of this novel will go to breast cancer prevention.
A stellar anthology that had me laughing, sighing in pleasure, believing in magic, and left me begging for more! Will there be a second anthology someday? I sure hope so! This is one novel that will go directly to my 'Keeper' shelf, to be read over and over again. Very highly recommended!

~ Detra Fitch, Huntress Reviews

***

LOVE UNDER THE MISTLETOE is a fun anthology that infuses the beauty of the season with fun characters and unforgettable situations. This is one of those books that you can read year round and still derive great pleasure from each of the charming stories. A Wonderful compilation of holiday stories. Perfect year round!
~ Chrissy Dionne, Romance Junkies

* * *

Brynn Chapman

*Cover by: Deborah MacGillivray
and Monika Wolmarans*

The Bride of Blackbeard

Brynn Chapman

Lightning Source UK Ltd.
Milton Keynes UK
UKOW052314150312

189030UK00001B/70/P